"WHAT'S IT LIKE, BEING THE FIRST KLINGON IN STARFLEET?"

Major Kira asked from the pilot's seat. Lieutenant Commander Worf sighed.

"That is the question that everyone asks," he replied coldly.

"I undertand," Kira said. "Every Bajoran I meet asks me what it's like to work with the Emissary."

"Oh?" Worf was curious.

Kira shrugged. "I tell them, 'it's a living.'"

Worf made a sound that in a human would have been called a sigh.

"I was raised by human parents," he told Kira, "so I grew up with Starfleet. Had my Klingon parents lived, I would no doubt be with my brothers now, helping to seize Cardassian Territory."

"You don't seem thrilled by that idea."

Worf shrugged. "It is a living. . . ."

Look for STAR TREK Fiction from Pocket Books

Star Trek: The Original Series

The Ashes of Eden
Federation
Sarek
Best Destiny
Shadows on the Sun
Probe
Prime Directive
The Lost Years
Star Trek VI: The Undiscovered Country
Star Trek V: The Final Frontier
Star Trek IV: The Voyage Home
Spock's World
Enterprise
Strangers from the Sky
Final Frontier

#1 Star Trek: The Motion Picture
#2 The Entropy Effect
#3 The Klingon Gambit
#4 The Covenant of the Crown
#5 The Prometheus Design
#6 The Abode of Life
#7 Star Trek II: The Wrath of Khan
#8 Black Fire
#9 Triangle
#10 Web of the Romulans
#11 Yesterday's Son
#12 Mutiny on the Enterprise
#13 The Wounded Sky
#14 The Trellisane Confrontation
#15 Corona
#16 The Final Reflection
#17 Star Trek III: The Search for Spock
#18 My Enemy, My Ally
#19 The Tears of the Singers
#20 The Vulcan Academy Murders
#21 Uhura's Song
#22 Shadow Lord
#23 Ishmael
#24 Killing Time
#25 Dwellers in the Crucible
#26 Pawns and Symbols
#27 Mindshadow
#28 Crisis on Centaurus
#29 Dreadnought!
#30 Demons
#31 Battlestations!
#32 Chain of Attack

#33 Deep Domain
#34 Dreams of the Raven
#35 The Romulan Way
#36 How Much for Just the Planet?
#37 Bloodthirst
#38 The IDIC Epidemic
#39 Time for Yesterday
#40 Timetrap
#41 The Three-Minute Universe
#42 Memory Prime
#43 The Final Nexus
#44 Vulcan's Glory
#45 Double, Double
#46 The Cry of the Onlies
#47 The Kobayashi Maru
#48 Rules of Engagement
#49 The Pandora Principle
#50 Doctor's Orders
#51 Enemy Unseen
#52 Home Is the Hunter
#53 Ghost Walker
#54 A Flag Full of Stars
#55 Renegade
#56 Legacy
#57 The Rift
#58 Face of Fire
#59 The Disinherited
#60 Ice Trap
#61 Sanctuary
#62 Death Count
#63 Shell Game
#64 The Starship Trap
#65 Windows on a Lost World
#66 From the Depths
#67 The Great Starship Race
#68 Firestorm
#69 The Patrian Transgression
#70 Traitor Winds
#71 Crossroad
#72 The Better Man
#73 Recovery
#74 The Fearful Summons
#75 First Frontier
#76 The Captain's Daughter
#77 Twilight's End
#78 The Rings of Tautee
#79 Invasion 1: First Strike
#80 The Joy Machine

Star Trek: The Next Generation

Kahless
Star Trek Generations
All Good Things
Q-Squared
Dark Mirror
Descent
The Devil's Heart
Imzadi
Relics
Reunion
Unification
Metamorphosis
Vendetta
Encounter at Farpoint

#1 Ghost Ship
#2 The Peacekeepers
#3 The Children of Hamlin
#4 Survivors
#5 Strike Zone
#6 Power Hungry
#7 Masks
#8 The Captains' Honor
#9 A Call to Darkness
#10 A Rock and a Hard Place
#11 Gulliver's Fugitives
#12 Doomsday World
#13 The Eyes of the Beholders
#14 Exiles

#15 Fortune's Light
#16 Contamination
#17 Boogeymen
#18 Q-in-Law
#19 Perchance to Dream
#20 Spartacus
#21 Chains of Command
#22 Imbalance
#23 War Drums
#24 Nightshade
#25 Grounded
#26 The Romulan Prize
#27 Guises of the Mind
#28 Here There Be Dragons
#29 Sins of Commission
#30 Debtors' Planet
#31 Foreign Foes
#32 Requiem
#33 Balance of Power
#34 Blaze of Glory
#35 Romulan Stratagem
#36 Into the Nebula
#37 The Last Stand
#38 Dragon's Honor
#39 Rogue Saucer
#40 Possession
#41 Invasion 2: The Soldiers of Fear
#42 Infiltrator
#43 A Fury Scorned

Star Trek: Deep Space Nine

Warped
The Search
#1 Emissary
#2 The Siege
#3 Bloodletter
#4 The Big Game
#5 Fallen Heroes
#6 Betrayal
#7 Warchild
#8 Antimatter

#9 Proud Helios
#10 Valhalla
#11 Devil in the Sky
#12 The Laertian Gamble
#13 Station Rage
#14 The Long Night
#15 Objective Bajor
#16 Invasion 3: Time's Enemy
#17 The Heart of the Warrior

Star Trek: Voyager

#1 Caretaker
#2 The Escape
#3 Ragnarok
#4 Violations
#5 Incident at Arbuk
#6 The Murdered Sun
#7 Ghost of a Chance
#8 Cybersong
#9 Invasion 4: The Final Fury
#10 Bless the Beasts

STAR TREK
DEEP SPACE NINE®

THE HEART OF
THE WARRIOR

John Gregory Betancourt

POCKET BOOKS

New York   London   Toronto   Sydney   Tokyo   Singapore

An *Original* Publication of POCKET BOOKS

POCKET BOOKS, a division of Simon & Schuster Inc.
1230 Avenue of the Americas, New York, NY 10020

STAR TREK is a Registered Trademark of Paramount Pictures.

A VIACOM COMPANY

This book is published by Pocket Books, a division of Simon & Schuster Inc., under exclusive license from Paramount Pictures.

ISBN: 0-671-00239-2

First Pocket Books printing October 1996

10 9 8 7 6 5 4 3 2 1

POCKET and colophon are registered trademarks of Simon & Schuster Inc.

Printed in the U.S.A.

This book is for
Virginia Kidd,
one of the sweetest people ever to grace
the science fiction field.

And for Kim,
my wonderful wife,
who makes everything possible.

HISTORIAN'S NOTE

The Trojan Spaceship takes place in the fourth season of STAR TREK: DEEP SPACE NINE.

THE HEART OF THE WARRIOR

CHAPTER
1

STATION LOG, CAPTAIN Benjamin Sisko, Arconina.

The Valtusian peace conference is scheduled to begin in two days aboard DS9. The Valtusians have managed the near impossible through tireless behind-the-scenes work, persuading not only representatives of the Cardassian government, but Maquis and Federation representatives to sit down together in the hopes of finally settling the Maquis problem.

Complicating logistics will be the loss of three key station personnel: Major Kira, Lieutenant Commander Worf, and Security Chief Odo, who are being dispatched on a high-priority mission into the Gamma Quadrant one day before the conference begins . . .

* * *

Major Kira Nerys leaned forward as far as she could, gazing out the vast curve of the Promenade's viewport toward the docking ring. She felt a growing sense of anticipation as she scanned the ships attached to the space station's outermost section for the one at Docking Pylon 7. She gazed past a beautiful new planet-hopper at Docking Pylon 5, past an old but serviceable Bajoran cargo carrier at Docking Pylon 6, and then found herself staring at an ancient, battered-looking transport ship parked just beyond them.

The moment she saw it, she thought she'd made a mistake. That hunk of junk couldn't possibly be their ship. Quickly she began counting out around the docking ring, and once again she came to the same broken-down wreck in Docking Port 7. What was Quark trying to do, get them all killed? A flash of rage passed through her, and she struggled to keep her temper under control. This wasn't anything like the sleek, fast little starship she'd been led to expect.

The transport ship had to be at least fifty years old. Its hull held hundreds if not thousands of pockmarks from collisions with space debris, and more than a couple of phaser burns scarred the nacelles, which hunched over the passenger cabin. One such burn had been sloppily patched with what looked like scrap iron. She leaned closer, straining to make out the details. Not durasteel, she thought, appalled, and not even regular steel—raw scrap iron.

I'm going to strangle him, she thought, gripping the railing as though it were the Ferengi's scrawny little neck. *There's no doubt about it this time. I'm going to strangle him.*

She felt the hair on the back of her neck bristle with indignation. She had suspected Quark would try to pull a fast one, and of course he had. When would Sisko learn not to deal with him? Trusting a Ferengi to get a civilian ship for them—it was nothing short of suicidal.

She shook her head in disgust and released the railing. "He can't be serious," she said, turning to Chief O'Brien beside her. She pointed at the ship. "Tell me that's not it!"

O'Brien frowned as he peered at the note in his hand. "Docking Port 7," he read. "That's her, all right. Perhaps she's not as bad as she looks."

"Right." She gave a derisive snort. "It's going to be ten times worse."

"We won't know till we look inside," O'Brien went on. His words sounded forced even to Kira.

"Come on, then," she said, turning toward the turbolift. "Let's get it over with so we can start looking for a real ship."

She wove her way through the crowds on the Promenade toward the nearest lift, letting her anger build to a white-hot fury. The station was packed, and crowds swelled the Promenade to bursting, but she noticed that everyone who saw her face or met her gaze had the good sense to scramble out of her way. *I never was very good at hiding my feelings,* she thought. *At least Quark won't mistake my reaction to his ship.*

She'd known Quark for quite a few years, and

though he'd always cut corners in his rush to make a profit, this was the most blatant rip-off she'd ever seen him try to pull. It bordered on criminal. And he had nerve to pull it on her—on all the station's command personnel! Well, he wasn't going to get away with it, she vowed, quickening her pace. She'd see to that.

The turbolift doors opened as she approached, and a pair of Vulcans in dark cloaks strolled out, gazing around with faintly curious expressions. They had probably come to monitor the peace conference, she thought . . . not that she had much hope for success. It had taken her people decades to wrest freedom from Cardassia. How could the Maquis expect success practically overnight? She nodded politely to the Vulcans and entered the turbolift, with O'Brien right on her heels.

"Docking ring," she snapped to the computer. The doors whisked closed, and they rode out in silence.

"Perhaps . . ." O'Brien mused.

Kira glanced at him and was shocked to find an intrigued look on his face. She'd never been great at reading people, but there couldn't be any mistaking his expression.

"You're thinking of taking that ship, aren't you?" she demanded.

"Uh . . . well, I'd have to have a closer look first, of course," he said, shifting a little uncomfortably. A hint of a blush crept into his cheeks. "It's not what's outside that counts, after all—"

"Forget it! Just forget it!" Kira said, waving her

arms for emphasis. Had everyone on the station gone crazy? "It's not going to happen! There's no way I'm going off to the Gamma Quadrant in that pile of junk!"

The lift door opened before O'Brien could answer, and Kira whirled and strode out angrily into the bustle of travelers, cargo handlers, and station personnel. DS9 never seemed to sleep anymore, she thought, and with the peace conference coming up, ships were arriving at a dizzying rate. Every berth on the docking ring was occupied, and more sat waiting in queue to disburse passengers and cargo. Dax and half the Ops staff were busy juggling schedules to make sure everyone got aboard the station in a timely manner.

She paused and glanced up and down the broad curve of the docking ring. Where was that Ferengi bastard? With so much going on, he had to be here.

Kira finally spotted Quark and his brother Rom standing off to one side talking to a pair of Andorians. The Andorians kept glancing around nervously; they seemed to be trying to keep a low profile, Kira thought. Although they wore long, concealing brown tunics with simple brass-colored belts, their shocks of white hair, bright blue skins, and antennae stood out in sharp contrast to everything around them.

Close by them, she noticed a pair of Bajoran cargo handlers in one-piece red uniforms lounging inconspicuously, as though on break. I know those two, she realized, and then managed to place their faces. They were two of Odo's deputies. They had to be keeping

Quark under surveillance, Kira thought with a touch of glee . . . leave it to Odo. Even with all the bustle going on, the constable still had time to keep tabs on the station's number one suspect.

Surveillance or not, she had her own problems with Quark right now, and she wasn't about to wait for him to finish his business with the Andorians. She stalked forward. The Andorians spotted her, muttered something to Quark, and hastily turned and walked farther up the docking ring. Probably smugglers, Kira thought with distaste; Quark would deal with anyone or anything if it meant profit. Still, she would trust Odo to keep him in check.

Her thoughts turned to the ship he was trying to foist off on them, and again her anger boiled up. *I can handle this,* she told herself. *I will not strangle him. Yet.*

"Quark—" she began, drawing to a halt in front of him.

"Major Kira!" Quark said, grinning happily. "Your ship has just arrived, exactly as ordered. And what a beauty, too—the *Galactic Queen,* a pleasure cruiser serving the Orjax Cluster until two weeks ago. Why, she only has fifty million light-years on her warp engines—"

Kira clenched her jaw. *I'm not going to strangle him,* she told herself again. She opened her mouth to give an angry retort, but O'Brien interrupted.

"And I'll bet," O'Brien said from behind her, "that she hasn't had a single day of regularly scheduled maintenance. We looked her over from the observa-

6

tion deck on the Promenade. We couldn't help but notice all the damage she's sustained over the years."

"Decades, rather," Kira muttered. Leave it to a human to try to play peacemaker, she thought. She gave O'Brien a displeased glance, but he flashed her a quick grin.

"A few minor cosmetic blemishes . . ." Quark began, giving them both a reassuring smile. "A little paint and you won't even know the difference. Isn't that right, Rom?"

"True, brother," Rom said quickly. "A little paint is all she needs."

"There you have it," Quark said with a winning smile.

"Paint." Kira folded her arms and contented herself with leveling a piercing stare at the little Ferengi. It seemed to work, she noticed with some satisfaction; Quark shifted uneasily from foot to foot.

"You won't find a better ship," he said.

"Come on," O'Brien said, holding out one hand. "Let's get it over with. I need the technical specs and the registration papers."

"Of course." Quark held out his palm and Rom slapped a datachip into it. Quark passed the chip over to O'Brien, then turned and led the way toward Airlock 7, saying, "She's a Delphi-class transport ship. As you no doubt already noticed, she is built using the finest Thelorian construction from human blueprints, with only fifty million light-years on her warp engines—"

"It won't do," Kira said flatly. Quark could talk it

up until his tongue fell out, but it didn't change one simple fact: The ship was a disaster. "For one thing, we need an airtight hull."

"Delphi-class?" O'Brien said, nodding. "I thought so. I worked on a couple of Delphi-class ships during the Cardassian war."

Delphi-class? Was that important? Kira glanced over at him. O'Brien's forehead had wrinkled in thought again. What was so great about a Delphi-class ship? It was just another obsolete model, as far as she knew. Wasn't it?

"That's right," Quark said smoothly, "a classic, isn't that so, Rom?"

"Right, brother," Rom said, rubbing his hands together nervously. "They don't make them like that anymore."

Kira gave a snort. "I can see why," she said. "It's a death trap."

Reaching the proper airlock, Quark punched an access code into the hand pad, then stood back as the huge red door rolled to the side like a cog in some vast clockwork mechanism.

Instantly a dank, wet, unpleasant odor flowed out through the airlock. Kira gagged and took a step back.

"What the hell is that stink?" she demanded, covering her nose and mouth with one hand. It had to be coming from inside the ship, she thought. What was Quark trying to do, poison them on top of everything else?

The smell got worse. Gasping, Kira retreated a couple of meters. It smelled like rotting meat and raw sewage mixed together, she thought, fighting down bile. She'd never smelled anything quite so foul.

Quark, too, was covering his nose. "Rom?" he demanded. "What's the meaning of this?"

"Brother, I think they mentioned a small problem with the ship's air filtration system," Rom said. "I'm sure I can fix it."

"No problem, then," Quark said. He turned back to O'Brien and gave a nervous little laugh. "Rom can fix it later tonight. Shall we look inside?"

"Close it up," O'Brien said, frowning and covering his own mouth and nose. "I'm not going in there with anything less than an environment suit!"

Quark punched in the code again and the door rolled shut. "Rom will get right on it," he promised.

"This ship is not even *remotely* acceptable," Kira said. She continued to fight down nausea. "You'll have to do better, Quark, if you expect to make a deal."

"It's the only thing on the market!" Quark protested. "You should see what I turned down to get this beauty for you—"

"It'll do," O'Brien said. He was nodding to himself and smiling faintly.

Kira gaped at him. *"What?"* she demanded. She could barely believe what she'd just heard. "How can you say that! This is a . . . a . . ." Words failed her. She didn't know where to begin.

"Prize?" Quark suggested. "Bargain?"

"It's no prize," O'Brien said, "but it just might do. If the systems check out, that is," he added hastily.

"I'll get back up here with a team in environment suits to look everything over in half an hour." He nodded toward the turbolift. "Come on, Major. Let's talk to the captain about it."

Kira set her feet. "Are you insane?" she demanded. She had no intention of accepting the ship. "It's a disaster waiting to happen!"

"Come *on,* Major," O'Brien said, still softly but more intensely. He gave a jerk of his head toward the lift. "Let's see the captain first, okay?"

She shrugged in despair. What was going through O'Brien's mind? Either he had a plan or he really *had* gone insane, she decided. If it was a plan, it had better be a damn good one.

"All right," she said. "We'll talk to the captain."

O'Brien started for the lift, and Kira trailed after him. How he could even *suggest* accepting this ship was beyond her. She puzzled over it. More than once she'd decided all humans were crazy, but there always seemed to be a method to their madness. Even so, O'Brien couldn't possibly accept such a pitiful excuse for a ship . . . could he? He hadn't even checked out the interior systems. Didn't he care about them? Didn't he at least want an airtight hull?

"Another pair of satisfied customers," Kira overheard Quark saying proudly to Rom.

That did it. She whirled, leveling another piercing glare at him. "Don't think this is over, Quark," she called. "Captain Sisko still has to sign off on the ship." And if I have my way, she mentally added, Odo will lock you up in that stinking hull for the rest of your life for trying to cheat us. Let the punishment fit the crime!

She hurried to join O'Brien in the turbolift. The second the doors shut, she demanded, "Are you *insane?* That ship—"

"Give me ten minutes at a comm station," he said, "and I'll let you know."

CHAPTER
2

"JUST ONE SMALL adjustment." Dr. Julian Bashir hid his nervousness behind a studied expression of calm. He flipped open the back panel of his new DNA analyzer, which he'd designed and built with the help of the station's computer. He bent down and peered inside at the complex tangle of circuits and relays and power couplings. What was wrong with it? It should be working. He'd gone over it a hundred times already, and every circuit checked out perfectly.

He glanced up at Captain Sisko. His commanding officer was frowning with impatience. Sisko's new beard and shaved head only emphasized that expression. Bashir swallowed. *I'd better finish up in a hurry,* he thought. Sisko was a busy man, juggling the Valtusian peace conference and a mission into the Gamma Quadrant, and he didn't have time to waste.

Behind Sisko, Lieutenant Commander Worf and Security Chief Odo both looked on with bored, slightly put-upon expressions. Worf sighed audibly and shifted from foot to foot. *I'm losing them,* Bashir thought.

Nevertheless, he continued to keep his expression a careful neutral as he examined the delicate microconnections inside the scanner. It *should* be working, he thought. Why wasn't it? He simply didn't understand the problem.

"Doctor . . ." Sisko began.

"One second more." His training at Starfleet Academy hadn't just covered biology and medicine. Bedside—in this case, *tableside*—manners were just as important, he knew. Like they said at Starfleet, as long as you look like you know what you're doing, your patients will have faith in you. Of course, he'd have to make sure that faith wasn't misplaced.

He sucked in a deep breath. The scanner *had* to work. Everything from the schematics to the programming parameters had checked out perfectly during computer-simulated tests. So why wouldn't it power up now?

Then he spotted the problem. It was so simple, he could have slapped himself. One power coupling had worked its way loose. He must have failed to lock it into position when he was assembling it, he realized. Carefully he reached in with two fingers, fitted it into the proper position, and pushed gently. He felt the two pieces lock together with a faint *snap.*

That should do it, he thought with a mental sigh of relief. He hoped.

"Well?" Sisko prompted.

Bashir smiled with new confidence as he stood up again. It *would* work, he told himself. You didn't graduate second in your class from Starfleet Academy without learning a thing or two about machines.

"Ready," he said.

He closed the DNA analyzer's back panel. Running one hand nervously through his short brown hair, he took a deep breath, then for the second time touched the activation button. *Now work, damn it,* he mentally instructed the machine. He willed it to start with every fiber of his being.

A low hum spread through the medical bay. Bashir slowly let out the breath he hadn't realized he'd been holding. It had powered up, he thought triumphantly. It was working. The power coupling hadn't been quite in place, that was all. It had been his own fault, not the machine's . . . simple human error.

"That fixed it," he said. "Sorry about the delay. Commander, if you wouldn't mind?"

Worf stepped forward. "What exactly do you want me to do?" the tall Klingon asked, his voice a low growl. He sounded a little nervous, Bashir thought. Klingons were just like human patients in that respect. They all had to be coddled and encouraged when it came to visiting sickbay. Sometimes he thought every intelligent life-form in the galaxy had an inborn distrust of the medical profession.

"Simply place your hand on top," he said. He

pushed the gray box toward Worf, giving him a reassuring smile. Best tableside manner and all that. "The scanner will do the rest."

Worf hesitated a second, glancing first at Captain Sisko, then at Odo. Slowly, tentatively, he reached out.

"You won't feel a thing," Bashir said encouragingly. At this rate it was going to take all afternoon.

"I am not afraid of pain," Worf said sharply. He slapped his hand down hard on top of the DNA scanner. The slap made a sharp *crack* loud enough to make a few of the nurses on the other side of the room jump.

Bashir winced a bit. Luckily the DNA scanner didn't seem to have been injured; it continued to hum along smoothly.

"Sorry," Worf said a little more meekly.

"No harm done," Bashir said. "I didn't mean to imply that you were afraid of pain," he added. One difference between Klingon and human patients, he realized, was that most human patients couldn't break you in half if you got them angry. "I simply meant that the process is painless."

The display panel on the side of the DNA scanner flashed twice. "Reading," it said, its computer voice faint and tinny. "Subject DNA passed. Subject is Klingon."

Worf withdrew his hand. Slowly he flexed his fingers, staring at them as though he thought they might have been changed. No chance of that, though, Bashir thought. It had removed a single skin cell with a microlaser.

"Very impressive, Doctor," Sisko said. "Now let's try a human."

"Shall I?" Bashir asked, starting to pull up his right sleeve.

"No. I'd like to try it myself."

Sisko placed his own hand on the scanner. After a second's analysis, the computer announced, "Subject DNA passed. Subject is human."

Sisko nodded. "Now it's your turn, Doctor," he said, stepping back and folding his arms.

Bashir stepped forward. The captain undoubtedly wanted to confirm that none of the command staff had been replaced by changelings, and he was happy to oblige. *Bashir's DNA Scanner to the rescue,* he thought. When he published a paper on the device, he was certain it would rapidly become the de facto standard in testing for changeling infiltration. *A work of near genius, if I do say so myself,* he thought with satisfaction.

He put his own hand on the scanner, and after a second it announced that he, too, was human. Of course.

That just left Odo. Bashir glanced at the station's changeling security officer. This, he thought, would be the real test.

"Your turn, Constable," Sisko said.

Without a moment's hesitation, Odo stepped forward and put his hand on top of the box just as the others had done.

"Reading," the device said.

Bashir leaned forward expectantly. Anyone could detect DNA in carbon-based life-forms. But detecting a changeling . . .

"Subject has no DNA," his DNA analyzer announced. "Subject is not a carbon-based life-form."

"Quite true," Odo said. "But what if they try to sneak aboard by impersonating a life-form that doesn't use DNA? Wouldn't that fool your device?"

"Some variant of DNA appears to be a universal constant in all carbon-based life-forms," Bashir said. "The Federation has only encountered a handful of silicon-based life-forms, like the Hortas, and none of them are likely to be on the station during these peace negotiations. Valtusians, Cardassians, Bajorans, all the races making up the Maquis, and in fact every carbon-based race that belongs to the Federation has a DNA signature on file with Starfleet Medical." He patted the top of the DNA analyzer proudly. "If changelings have replaced one or more of them, we'll know it, believe me."

"And since we're pulling this test as a surprise, they won't have any chance to prepare any sort of countermeasure," Sisko said.

"I doubt that's possible—" Bashir began, but Odo interrupted.

"Don't underestimate my people," he said. "Remember what they did on Earth."

Bashir nodded, then swallowed. They had indeed infiltrated Starfleet Command and the Federation headquarters, even going so far as blowing up a conference with the Romulans. Starfleet had lost many key personnel. The changelings were crafty and resourceful. In time, they might indeed find some way around his device . . . but hopefully not before he smoked out any spies aboard DS9.

The captain's badge chirped. "Sisko here," he said.

"Benjamin," Lieutenant Jadzia Dax's voice said, "the Valtusian ambassadors have arrived. I'm routing them to Docking Pylon Three. I thought you might want to welcome them aboard."

"Thank you, Dax," he said. "I'm on my way." He glanced at Bashir and said, "Doctor, I believe it's time to field test your DNA scanner."

"Right," Bashir said with a grin. This was what he'd been waiting for, after all.

"And, Constable," Sisko went on, "I think you should join us as well. And you too, Mr. Worf, if you're willing."

"Certainly," Odo said.

"Agreed," Worf said.

Bashir picked up his DNA analyzer and tucked it under his arm. He'd never met a Valtusian before, though of course he knew their reputation as a race of tinkerers and philosophers. Few of them left Valtusia, preferring to live in their own communal villages, pondering the universe, writing poetry, tinkering with intricate clockwork mechanisms, and devoting themselves to the mysteries of their kind. This should prove most interesting, he thought.

CHAPTER 3

As soon as Kira and O'Brien were out of sight, Quark rubbed his hands together with satisfaction. They were going to buy his ship. He had that tingling sensation in his lobes that meant a deal was going perfectly. He smiled, thinking of the latinum to come. First the ship, then the peace conference. He could look forward to record profits this month. He chuckled. Yes, things were certainly going well.

"I don't understand—" Rom began.

"That's why I'm in charge," Quark replied smugly. "Remember the one hundred and third Rule of Acquisition."

"'Fill a desperate need with your most expensive product, then mark it up five hundred percent?'" Rom's brow furrowed. "I still don't understand, brother."

Quark sighed. His brother might be a mechanical genius, but he still needed someone to hold his hand during complicated business deals. "You may recall some pilgrims from Arvanus Six who ended up stranded here six months ago," he began. "They came—"

"In a Delphi-class starship!" Rom finished. Quark saw the realization in his brother's eyes. "It's still there, on the seventh Bajoran moon!"

"If *I* remembered that fact, I knew Chief O'Brien would, too," Quark said smugly. "The pilgrims' ship doesn't have working warp engines, but the passenger compartment should be fine. It shouldn't take O'Brien and his men long to assemble one working ship out of the two. Because it's such a perfect match, I quadrupled my original asking price for the *Galactic Queen.*" He patted the airlock affectionately. "A small fortune, Rom, and it's all mine!"

"Brilliant," Rom breathed. "But I believe you're forgetting something."

"What?"

"My cut, brother! In exchange for my technical help, you promised—"

"A fortune less five percent is still a fortune," Quark said, waving one hand dismissively. Rom never seemed to grasp such fundamentals of business. "Come on, let's get back to the bar before the Dabo girls rob me blind."

In Ops, Major Kira leaned against one of the consoles and watched as Chief O'Brien fed a series of queries into the computer. Maybe humans weren't crazy after all, she thought, as the information began to trickle back out.

The first thing O'Brien looked at was the station's recording of the *Galactic Queen*'s warp signature as it entered Bajoran space. It appeared completely normal, which meant the ship's warp engines worked within acceptable parameters. It seemed almost miraculous, considering the otherwise deplorable condition of the *Galactic Queen*.

"All right," Kira said, "the engines work. But what about everything else? What about the hull—that stench is enough to smother anyone!"

"I'm getting to that." He punched up a series of salvage records and began scanning them. Kira shook her head in bewilderment. They weren't even the *Galactic Queen*'s records—they belonged to another ship, this one called the *Progress*. Crazy, indeed.

"Just as I thought," O'Brien said suddenly. "There's still a Delphi-class ship sitting on the seventh Bajoran moon. It hasn't been picked up for salvage yet."

"The pilgrims . . ." Kira said, suddenly remembering the problems that had left them stranded on DS9 with no way back to Arvanus VI six months previously. That had been one logistical nightmare, all right. Luckily Captain Sisko had been able to arrange transport home for them aboard a freighter. She frowned, thinking back to the incident. What had been wrong with their ship? It had been their warp engines, she recalled. They had damaged their warp core and fried both nacelles.

She snapped her fingers, suddenly putting two and two together. "Quark's ship has working engines," she said.

"That's right." O'Brien leaned back in his chair and laced his fingers behind his head, grinning widely. "Still think I'm crazy, Major?"

She could have laughed with relief. "No. But can you assemble one working ship out of the pair?"

"If the engines are in decent shape aboard Quark's ship—and I suspect they are from the warp signature—I can have them out and fitted aboard the pilgrims' *Progress* in six hours. The Delphi-class is modular. I've done it before."

"Then our only problem," Kira said, sliding into the seat next to O'Brien, "will be acquiring salvage rights to the pilgrims' ship." She transferred the salvage claim he'd been studying to her terminal. "Loran Devys Salvage," she read aloud, "owns the hull."

The name sounded familiar. Where did she know Loran from? Suddenly it came to her. There had been a fellow named Loran Devys in another cell during the resistance. She'd worked with him at least once. If this was the same man, perhaps he'd remember her and cut her a deal. It was worth a try, anyway.

"Do you think you can get the rights to it?" O'Brien was saying.

"There's only one way to find out." She opened a

link to Bajor and called the number on the salvage claim.

A Bajoran woman in a gold and silver one-piece suit answered. An intricate earring dangled from her right ear. "Loran Devys Salvage," she said, then her eyes widened. "Nerys!" she said in surprise.

Kira forced a smile. "That's right," she said. Who was this woman? She didn't look familiar.

"You don't remember me, of course," the woman said. "I'm Jael—Koratta Jael, from Devys's cell? We only met once, and it was many years ago. But I've seen you quite a few times lately on the news reports. You're making quite a name for yourself. Are you still stationed on DS9?"

"Yes," Kira said. Koratta Jael . . . that name did sound vaguely familiar, even if her face wasn't. It had been quite a few years, she reminded herself. People could change a lot in all that time. She tried to think back to the others in Devys's cell. "Didn't you used to have your hair . . ." she began, sketching vaguely with her hands.

Koratta was nodding. "Yes, much longer. You do remember. It's wonderful to talk to you again, Nerys, but is this a social call?"

"I'm afraid it's business," Kira said. "Devys owns salvage rights to a Delphi-class transport ship on the seventh Bajoran moon. Perhaps you know the one I'm talking about."

"We own a lot of salvage. Wait a second." Jael punched something up on her computer terminal.

"Yes, I see the one you mean. The *Progress,* a Delphi-class transport. We picked it up at auction six weeks ago. It's scheduled for retrieval next month."

"I'd like to buy it," Kira said.

Jael stared at her in surprise. "It's a dead hull," she said. "No power—"

"I know," Kira said, and quickly she explained that they hoped to assemble one whole ship out of two. "Do you think Devys might be willing to sell it to me?"

"I'm sure he would," Koratta said, studying the records before her. "We have the estimated salvage value as scrap duranium at twenty-two bars of gold-pressed latinum. If you'd like to buy it, that would be the price. Frankly, I'm sure he'd jump at the offer—it would save us a lot of work."

"Thanks, Jael," Kira said with a smile she truly felt this time. The price sounded more than fair to her. At times like these, she thought the resistance movement had brought the Bajoran people closer together than at any other time in history. "Hold the ship for me. I'll get back to you later today to work out the details."

"Of course," Jael said. "I'm happy to help. Take care of yourself, Nerys." She severed the connection.

Kira leaned back. "It looks like we've got your hull," she said a trifle smugly to O'Brien. It was easy, when you knew the right people.

O'Brien shook his head. "Is there anyone you don't know on Bajor?" he asked.

Kira grinned. Sometimes it felt that way to her, too.

"You forget how big the resistance movement was, Chief."

He rose suddenly. "I'd better get an environment suit and take a look at the *Galactic Queen*'s engines," he said. "I'll let you know in half an hour whether it's workable."

As the airlock cycled and the huge coglike door rolled to the side, Benjamin Sisko pulled his shirt smooth and drew himself up straighter. A Starfleet captain had to maintain an air of dignity at all times, he knew. The Valtusian delegation had gone to a lot of trouble to set up these peace negotiations, and Admiral Dulev had underlined the importance of success to him. Fighting the Maquis sapped both Cardassian and Federation strength, diverting their attention from a larger threat in the Gamma Quadrant. If there could be a fair and amicable settlement, they would jump on it.

If only the Valtusians' timing had been better. He didn't relish the idea of having this peace conference aboard DS9 while Odo, Kira, and Worf were away.

Their mission to the Gamma Quadrant had come about three days previously, when Admiral Dulev had summoned him to Starbase 201. He'd gone aboard the *Defiant* with Worf and Dax.

There, they had been ushered almost at once into the admiral's meeting room. It had been Spartanly furnished: a long table, eight chairs, a pitcher of ice water on a tray with glasses. Sisko surveyed the room and noticed the three other people already there and tried to hold in his surprise. The admiral, of course, sat at the head of the table. She had her brown hair pulled back in the severe bun that was becoming popular among high-ranking Starfleet women. To her right sat her golden boy, Lieutenant Colfax, looking a little smug in his trim red command uniform. To the admiral's left sat a humanoid alien covered in pale yellow fur, with a pronounced snout and eight-fingered hands . . . a female Groxxin, he realized. They were native to the Gamma Quadrant. So what was this one doing sitting in on Admiral Dulev's meeting?

The admiral wasted no time in getting down to business. "You remember Lieutenant Colfax, of course," she said. Sisko nodded; Colfax had been the one to contact him about this meeting. "This is Zheronn," she said, indicating the alien, "one of our informants from the Gamma Quadrant."

Sisko raised his eyebrows slightly, but made no comment. An informant would have to have big news to travel this far, he realized. It meant the Groxxin had abandoned her job, her family, and any cover she might have established to hide her activities.

"Zheronn," the admiral went on, leaning forward slightly, "has made a discovery about the labs which genetically engineered the Jem'Hadar for the changelings. It seems that these 'perfect warriors' are not quite so perfect as we thought."

"In what way?" Dax asked, leaning forward with interest.

The admiral punched something into the terminal

to her right. Instantly a holographic projection appeared over the conference table: a common molecular sequence, Sisko saw as it revolved: a double-helix design. It looked almost like human genetic coding.

"The Jem'Hadar version of DNA?" Dax guessed.

"That's right," Admiral Dulev said. "The complete genetic code for the Jem'Hadar, including the changes which created their chemical dependency on the drug called Ketracel-white, their inborn respect for the Founders, and most important of all, their aggressively militant natures."

"Surely we had already had access to this information," Sisko said. "We've encountered the Jem'Hadar often enough to have skin and other cell samples available for our scientists to analyze."

"True. What we didn't have was a way to shut off these Founder-given genetic tweaks."

"Shut them off . . ." Sisko echoed, shocked. "You mean we can change their genetic code?"

"You're talking about a retrovirus, aren't you?" Dax asked. Sisko heard the rise of excitement in her voice. She knew what this meant, too, he thought.

"I do not follow you," Worf said.

Dax turned to him. "Retroviruses are small organisms that work on a genetic level. They exist as parasites in DNA. Your body is full of them, but that's all right since most of them are harmless. Some of the more dangerous types can rewrite bits of genetic code, making changes throughout the body."

"Like Panzer's Syndrome," Sisko said. His few medical classes at the Federation started coming back to him. A retrovirus had invaded the bodies of every colonist on Galagos VI, and two hundred thousand humans had suddenly found themselves developing gills as a dormant genetic code reactivated itself.

"Exactly," the admiral said. "I'll let Zheronn explain." She turned to the yellow-furred Groxxin.

Zheronn hesitated a second. When she spoke, the universal translator gave her a soft, sultry voice.

"My mate and I work at Laboratory Complex Ileph-B on Daborat V," she said. "We were in charge of cataloging and filing. One day a computer error gave us access to a classified section of the cataloging system, and Orvor found records from the earliest days of the Dominion including the designs for a retrovirus that can modify the Jem'Hadar's genetic code to eliminate their violent tendencies and stop their dependence on Ketracel-white. In essence, it returns them to their state before the Founders modified their bodies."

"Effectively neutralizing them as a military threat," Lieutenant Colfax finished.

"If that is true," Worf said, "we must obtain that retrovirus at all costs."

Sisko steepled his fingers thoughtfully. This sounded like the solution to their conflict with the changelings. Without the Jem'Hadar to back them up with military strength, much of the Dominion's threat to the Alpha Quadrant would be ended.

And yet something still bothered him. Why had they been summoned to this meeting? Where did he fit into Admiral Dulev's plan?

"Why do I feel there's a catch?" he asked.

Zheronn said, "Only one of us could make it out with the information, and Orvor chose to send me. He, however, kept the design specifications for the retrovirus. You must rescue him from Daborat V to get it. That is our price for helping you."

"Impossible," Worf said. "Daborat V is one of the most heavily guarded Jem'Hadar bases in the Gamma Quadrant!"

"It must be done," Zheronn said. "That is our price."

"We feel a small group may be able to infiltrate Daborat V successfully in order to bring Orvor out," Admiral Dulev said. "Your people have the most experience with changelings and the Jem'Hadar, Captain. I want you to put together an away team for this mission including your Constable Odo. They will depart as soon as possible. Time is of the essence."

Sisko frowned a bit. Rescuing someone from one of the largest Jem'Hadar bases in the Gamma Quadrant was a lot to ask, but he knew that with such a big payoff at stake, they had to take the chance.

He said, "I'll need a civilian ship."

"Requisition whatever you need," Admiral Dulev said, rising. "I'll leave you and Lieutenant Colfax to work out the details." She nodded to Zheronn, and the two of them left together.

As soon as they were alone, Lieutenant Colfax smiled his too-smooth smile and said in his too-smooth voice, "Who do you have in mind for this mission, Captain?"

And so Sisko had mentioned Kira and Worf. Worf had been only too happy to volunteer, as had Major Kira when he briefed her the following day back at DS9. Things had fallen quickly into place from there. If all went well, the three of them—Kira, Worf, and Odo—would leave tomorrow, and the peace negotiations would continue without pause aboard DS9.

The airlock door finished opening, and Sisko felt his ears pop slightly as the Valtusian ship released its seals and pressures equalized. Suddenly a scent of the ship's internal atmosphere reached Sisko, and he found himself breathing deeply. It was a rich, earthy smell, filled with the tang of nitrogen and ozone, and it made the skin on the back of his hands and neck prickle. It smelled just like New Orleans after a thunderstorm, he thought, enjoying the sensation. It brought back quite a few pleasant memories, and for an instant he wished he could visit his father again. *I do need a vacation,* he thought. *Maybe after everything settles down again.*

He forced his mind back to the here and now as three Valtusian ambassadors strolled single file through the airlock. All three had to duck—they towered over him, each a little more than two and a half meters in height, but less than half as wide as an average human. Their elongated gray-green skulls, the only part of their bodies showing, held two large, bulbous, unblinking green eyes set on either side of their heads. Their toothless mouths were oddly tiny, and they had no noses, only a pair of slits covered by a fine grayish green membrane that flared open, then closed, then flared open again as they breathed.

They had a dislike of physical contact, Sisko recalled, which probably explained the concealing robes. Even their hands were covered, he noticed. That wouldn't make Bashir's job any easier.

Their feet making faint clicking noises beneath their robes, they drew to a stop before him. Sisko swallowed as he gazed up at their leader's face. He hadn't realized they were so tall, and he tried not to stare. Of course he knew what they looked like from pictures, and many years ago he'd seen one on Vulcan in the distance, but it had not prepared him to meet three at one time. They were daunting, to say the least.

He glanced from one to another. It was impossible to tell which was their leader. As one, they bowed to him, their foreheads almost touching the floor.

Sisko bowed back and noted how Bashir and Odo did likewise. Worf, to their far left, nodded politely. They knew their protocols as well as he did.

"Welcome to *Deep Space Nine*," he began. "I am Captain Benjamin Sisko. This is my chief medical officer, Julian Bashir, and Constable Odo, who is in charge of security for the peace conference, and Lieutenant Commander Worf, my military operations officer. On behalf of the Federation, we wish to welcome you and extend an invitation to use any of the facilities aboard the station that you require."

The three Valtusians bowed again. "I am Ambassador Zhosh," said the one on the far left. His voice was high and reedy, almost musical. "My associates are Gerazh and Senosh."

"Do you have any special requirements to make your stay more pleasant?" Sisko asked. "The environmental control in your suites can be adjusted to suit your needs, of course, but if there is anything else . . .?"

"This has been a long and tiring journey," Ambassador Zhosh said. "We would like to rest now."

"Of course," Sisko said. "We have one small security formality, however. We are requiring all conference attendees to take a DNA screening test. This is entirely for your own safety, of course," he added.

"Test?" Ambassador Zhosh said. His solid green eyes stared unblinkingly at Sisko, and bits of gold inside them seemed to sparkle with sudden anger. "We were not informed of any such test."

"It is a routine security check, to make sure you are who you say you are," Sisko said quickly. He tried to keep his voice calm and soothing. He could well understand the ambassador's reaction; there weren't supposed to be any surprises in diplomacy. "As I am sure you're aware, there is the possibility of change-lings from the Gamma Quadrant trying to infiltrate and disrupt this peace conference."

"Yes," said Zhosh distantly. "We do understand the necessity. You may proceed."

"Doctor?" he said, moving aside. Bashir had a soothing manner when dealing with patients, he knew, and that was what the situation called for. The

Valtusians were an intensely private race, and he did not want to offend them.

Bashir stepped forward and held out his DNA analyzer. "This box will read your DNA and identify your genetic codes," he said, "then use them to verify that none of you is a changeling."

"How does it work?" Ambassador Zhosh asked, cocking his head to the side and staring down at the box with one round green eye.

"Place your hand on top of the device. It will remove a skin cell and analyze it."

Zhosh drew back as if horrified by the idea. "Our hands must not be touched!" he said with a shudder. There was a note of alarm in his voice. "Our hands must not be touched!"

They must have stumbled onto a cultural taboo, Sisko realized with a mental sigh. Perhaps that was why the Valtusians wrapped themselves so thoroughly in robes. That, or the Valtusians were changelings, which seemed singularly unlikely, since they had spearheaded the peace initiative from the beginning.

Quickly he said, "I'm sure we can work out an alternative testing method."

"It doesn't matter what part of the body is used," Bashir said hastily. "Arms, elbows, feet—any patch of skin will do."

Ambassador Zhosh gave another shudder. "We must discuss this matter privately," he said. "This is a serious breach of protocol, Captain Sisko. We are not pleased."

Turning, he led the other two Valtusians back into

their ship. The airlock door rolled closed with a low grating sound.

Sisko swallowed. Had he single-handedly derailed the peace process? If so, Admiral Dulev would have his head on a platter—not an event he looked forward to.

"I'm afraid they didn't react at all well to my scanner," Dr. Bashir said uneasily.

Worf said sharply, "They are hiding something."

"I felt that, too," Odo said.

"I don't know very much about them," Sisko admitted. "However, nothing I've seen here today is the least bit out of character. They *are* an intensely private people, after all, and we may have stumbled onto one of their taboos. Let's give them a few minutes to talk things over. After all, we did spring this on them as a surprise. What do you think, Constable?"

"I don't like them," Odo said. "Something about them makes me distinctly uneasy."

That was interesting, Sisko thought. Odo very rarely voiced his inner feelings. He had to be more than a little uneasy to speak up like this now.

"Why don't you call for more security," Sisko said, "in case we need help. Just keep them back. We don't want an incident if we can avoid one."

"Agreed." Odo tapped his badge and said, "Bring a security detachment to Docking Port Three on the double!"

Sisko tried to wait patiently. His thoughts bounced back and forth between the Valtusians, the peace conference, and the possibility of changelings trying to disrupt matters. Why weren't things ever easy?

Four of Odo's security guards arrived, panting a bit from sprinting, and Odo drew them aside, getting into position to cover the hatch unobtrusively. Hopefully it wouldn't be necessary, Sisko thought. Were the Valtusians ever coming out? How long would it take them to discuss the matter of being tested?

Sisko glanced at a chronometer. Only three minutes had passed, he told himself. That wasn't long to wait. He had to be patient—diplomats moved at their own pace, after all, and he didn't want to get off on the wrong foot by pushing too hard.

Suddenly the hatch rolled back and the three Valtusians emerged single file once more. Sisko frowned. What *was* that faint clicking sound? Ambassador Zhosh—at least Sisko *thought* it was Ambassador Zhosh—addressed him again.

"We have discussed the matter," Zhosh said, "and we will allow your device to touch us. It may analyze our feet, which are among the least sacred parts of our body."

Zhosh pulled up the hem of his flowing green robe, revealing a long, narrow green foot that ended in three clawed toes. A fourth and much broader claw jutted from its heel. The Valtusians walked balanced on the tips of the claws, Sisko realized, which explained the faint clicking he heard when they moved.

"That will do nicely," Dr. Bashir said.

He activated his DNA scanner and set it on the floor in front of Ambassador Zhosh. Sisko watched with interest as the Valtusian gave a birdlike hop forward and placed the flat middle part of its foot upon the box.

"Reading," the scanner said. It paused for a long time—longer than it had with Worf, Dr. Bashir, or Odo. Sisko took a deep breath . . . had it broken down again? If so, Bashir would have a lot of explaining to do.

But then the lights on its side flashed twice, and it said, "Subject DNA passed. Subject is Valtusian."

Sisko smiled to hide his relief, thinking of the time on Earth when he'd mistaken his own father for a changeling. His father had refused to take a blood test being administered to the families of all Federation officials due to plain old-fashioned stubbornness, nothing more, and Sisko had learned a lesson that day about paranoia. You had to have limits. Life wasn't worth living if you couldn't trust anyone around you. He nodded a bit. No, there weren't any changelings here—just the private mysteries of an alien race. Dr. Bashir wouldn't have these body-taboo problems with the humans or Cardassians attending the conference, at least.

"When are the other representatives scheduled to arrive?" Ambassador Zhosh asked, as Bashir ran the other two Valtusians through the test.

"The Cardassian delegation should be here in a few hours," Sisko said. "The Maquis and the Federation ambassadors are scheduled to arrive tomorrow."

"I have an itinerary prepared. We will begin in two days, at the ninth bell."

"The ninth bell?" Sisko repeated.

"That would be approximately eight-fifteen in the morning," Dr. Bashir said. The second ambassador passed the test. "The Valtusian calendar is quite interesting," he went on. "Their clocks use musical tones to indicate the time."

Sisko felt his eyes starting to glaze over as Dr. Bashir began one of his endless lectures, this one on Valtusian clockwork mechanisms. *He really should have gone into teaching,* Sisko thought. *The way he likes to talk, he would have made an excellent instructor at the Academy.* Then he reminded himself that he'd be losing one of the best doctors in Starfleet. *He can always retire to teaching,* he told himself.

"Quite correct." Zhosh gazed at Bashir with one eye. "Have you visited Valtusia, Doctor?"

"No, but my mother owns one of your clocks."

The third Valtusian also passed the test. Odo's suspicions had proved unfounded, for once. No changelings here.

"Ah." Ambassador Zhosh faced Sisko again. "If we could be shown to our quarters now?"

"Certainly," he began, and then his badge chirped. "One second," he told Zhosh. He tapped his badge. "Sisko here."

"I have a priority one transmission for you from Admiral Dulev," Dax said.

"Thank you," Sisko said. "I'll be right there." He turned back to Ambassador Zhosh. "Constable Odo will have to show you to the habitat ring," he said. "If you need anything, don't hesitate to let him know."

All three Valtusians bowed low to him. He returned the gesture, then hurried toward the turbolift.

"This way," Odo said behind him, sounding faintly irritated that they hadn't turned out to be changeling spies after all. "Right now we are in the third docking pylon," he said, beginning the standard tour of the station. "Your quarters will be in the habitat ring . . ."

"Ops," Sisko said to the computer as he entered the turbolift. It whisked him down rapidly. Another transmission from Admiral Dulev . . . what could she want?

CHAPTER 4

"ADMIRAL DULEV," SISKO said as her stern face appeared on his monitor. He couldn't recall ever seeing her smile.

"Captain Sisko," she said, as usual cutting through all formalities, "you are to delay the mission to the Gamma Quadrant until the *Excalibur* gets there."

"If I may ask," Sisko said, "why?"

"My aide, Lieutenant Colfax, will be aboard the *Excalibur*. He will brief you and your people fully upon his arrival."

"Very well," Sisko said, puzzled. "When is the *Excalibur* due?"

"Thirty-two hours. If you have any questions, please address them to Lieutenant Colfax. Dulev out," she said, and the screen went blank.

Sisko steepled his fingers thoughtfully. Thirty-two

hours. Starbase 201, where he'd met with the admiral and Colfax, lay sixteen hours away which meant the *Excalibur* either hadn't arrived yet or had another stop to make before coming to DS9. At least the extra time would give them a chance to better prepare for the mission into the Gamma Quadrant. The peace conference should already be underway by then. Perhaps it would be less of a juggling act than he thought. He could certainly use the extra help Odo would provide when the Cardassian delegation arrived.

Cardassians on the station always meant trouble, he knew . . . not that they themselves posed a threat to DS9's security. If anything, they tended toward model behavior while visiting. The problems always came from Bajorans, with their endless protests and picketing and threats of violence against any and all Cardassians they deemed war criminals.

He felt a slight headache beginning, and he forced himself to stretch and focus his eyes on the far wall. Too much work, too much stress—he'd better not let Dr. Bashir find out, or he'd find himself in a holosuite on forced R and R despite the importance of everything going on around him.

He picked up the baseball he kept on his desk and gripped it in his strong right hand. The tension of dealing with two high-priority missions simultaneously was starting to get to him, he thought. He needed to unwind. Perhaps a half hour game of catch with his son Jake, or in a holosuite with the 2106 Brooklyn Dodgers . . . a scenario he'd been working on for some weeks now. The Cardassians weren't due yet, the Valtusians were safely in their quarters, and the *Excalibur* wouldn't arrive for thirty-two hours. He'd have enough time, wouldn't he?

The door to his office chirped. Sighing, he put the baseball back on its little stand. No rest for a weary captain, he thought. "Come," he called.

Lieutenant Jadzia Dax stepped in. Behind her he could see Major Kira and Chief O'Brien. "Benjamin," Dax said, "if you have a minute . . ."

"Of course," he said, leaning back in his chair. "What is it, Dax? A problem with Quark's ship?"

"Have you been looking over my shoulder?" she asked with a faint smile.

"I expected it, actually," Sisko said. "What do you think, Chief? Will it do?"

"It's a death trap," O'Brien said.

"That doesn't sound very promising." *But probably what I should have expected,* he mentally added. They might have to use a runabout after all.

"It gets better," Dax said. "Quark has already billed us for two hundred and fifty bars of gold-pressed latinum."

"Outrageous," Sisko agreed, shaking his head. Still, what could he expect from a Ferengi?

"But here's the thing, sir," O'Brien said, leaning forward. "It's a Delphi-class ship, just like the one the pilgrims from Arvanus Six abandoned on the seventh Bajoran moon. The pilgrims' ship has already been claimed for salvage by a Bajoran company, but they haven't picked it up yet."

"I've made a few inquiries of my own," Kira added.

"We can have the pilgrim ship's hull for twenty-two bars of latinum. All it needs are new warp engines . . ."

"And Quark's ship has those," O'Brien finished.

Sisko looked at Dax. "What do you think?" he asked her.

She shook her head a fraction. "I think it's risky. We have one day to put together a working starship. That would be hard under the best of circumstances. But I don't see a better alternative."

"I have good news on that front," Sisko said. "Admiral Dulev wants the mission delayed until the *Excalibur* gets here. That gives us at least thirty-two hours."

"Is the *Excalibur* coming with us?" Kira asked.

"The admiral wasn't clear on that point," Sisko said. "I would assume not, though. So, what do you think, Chief? Can you put together a working ship for us in thirty-two hours?"

"Oh, we can do it." O'Brien nodded. "For once, I've got every system on DS9 functioning within acceptable parameters. It's taken me three years, but it's finally happened. I can put every man I have on refitting the warp engines. Delphi-class ships are completely modular in design, so it shouldn't be too hard. My original estimate was six hours, and I still think it can be done that quickly. The extra time will give us a chance to make a few shakedown flights and run full diagnostics."

"Excellent." Sisko considered the options. If

O'Brien said he could make a working ship out of the two, Sisko knew he could rely on him to deliver. Their three years here together had proved his chief engineer's competence time and again. Still, putting together a fix-up ship had its own risks. You never knew quite what you were getting with a used starship . . . let alone two of them. Systems might fail suddenly, or there might be slight design variations between them if they were built in different years.

Unfortunately, there didn't seem to be much choice. They needed a civilian ship, and there just weren't any available through regular channels on such short notice. He began to nod. It seemed Admiral Dulev's delay was in fact a godsend.

"Very well," he said, "get on it . . . as soon as I finish with Quark."

"Two hundred and fifty bars of gold-pressed latinum *is* an outrageous price for a ship in that condition," Dax said.

"What's fair?" Sisko asked, looking at O'Brien. He would know, if anyone did aboard DS9, because he kept close tabs on the used equipment market. "A hundred?"

"I'd say fifty," O'Brien said, "if that. It needs a lot of work."

Kira said, "Security has been keeping Quark under surveillance. Why don't you ask Odo what Quark paid for it?"

"An excellent suggestion, Major," Sisko said. *I must be slipping,* he thought. *I should have thought of that myself.* He activated the communications console on his desk, and a second later Odo's smooth, nearly featureless face appeared on the viewscreen.

"Yes, Captain?" Odo asked, sounding faintly annoyed. Sisko hid his smile. Everything seemed to faintly annoy Odo.

"Did you get the Valtusian ambassadors settled into their suite?" he asked.

"Yes." He sounded more annoyed than ever. "Was there anything else?"

"By any chance, can you tell me what Quark paid for that ship he just bought?"

"The *Galactic Queen*—if you can call that mess a ship?" Odo gave a snort. "He didn't pay anything for it. Two Andorians paid *him* to take it off their hands. Repairs would cost more that it's worth, and the owners couldn't even afford the station's docking fees. Quark promised to handle everything for them, including the disposal of their ship, for two bars of gold-pressed latinum."

Sisko had to laugh. "Leave it to Quark to try to make a profit on every side of a deal," he said.

"I don't find that particularly amusing," Odo said. "Am I missing something, sir?"

"Not really. Thank you, Constable. Keep up the good work." He shut off the viewscreen. "Well," he said to Dax and the others, "that certainly gives us a lot of bargaining room."

Kira folded her arms. "I say we let him keep the ship. We can still take a runabout."

"I wouldn't object if you weren't going to a planet

with a Jem'Hadar base," Sisko said. "Taking a Federation vessel is simply too risky. Besides, I think Quark's ship will work out, as soon as negotiations are over."

He turned again to his communications console. "Quark," he said, and a second later an image appeared on the viewscreen before him: Quark in his bar, the babble of happy crowds creating a pleasant background noise. Cheers came from one of the gambling tables, followed by cries of "Dabo!"

"Captain Sisko!" Quark said. He was wiping a glass clean. "This is an unexpected surprise. I take it Chief O'Brien has relayed the good news about the ship I found?"

"It is unacceptable," Sisko said, clipping his words to emphasize how seriously he took the matter. "We have had to make other arrangements, Quark. I'm very disappointed in you."

"What!" The shock was apparent on Quark's face. Sisko felt a sudden pang of sympathy, but forced it down. You had to play hardball with Ferengis during negotiations, as the old saying went. They'd walk all over you if you didn't.

"I'm sorry things didn't work out," he went on. "I'll let you know if we have any more needs." He disconnected, and Quark's face disappeared.

Smiling, Sisko leaned back in his seat and looked at his officers. "Bets?" he asked, taking a glance at the chronometer.

"Ten seconds," O'Brien said instantly.

"Ten? You're crazy," Kira said. "Eight."

"It'll take him that long just to stop shaking," Dax said. "Twelve, at least."

"I'll take fifteen," Sisko said.

The seconds ticked away. Eight . . . ten . . . and at twelve seconds exactly the communicator chirped.

"I believe you three owe me dinner," Dax said triumphantly.

Before Sisko could touch the controls, Quark's face appeared on the viewscreen. Sisko frowned, a trifle annoyed. The security devices in Ops and his private office shouldn't let calls through to him like that. Quark must have a security key. He made a mental note to have Odo confiscate it.

"Quark," Sisko said, trying to keep his tone even and pleasant. "What can I do for you?"

"About this ship—"

"It won't do. I thought we settled that."

"If it's a matter of price, I *am* open to reasonable counteroffers."

Sisko shook his head. "As I told you, time is of the essence here. Chief O'Brien informs me that it will take all of his people two days working around the clock to get that ship put back into working order. I simply cannot spare him at this time, with the peace conference coming up, so I have been forced to make other arrangements. Luckily I managed to find an alternate ship through an old friend of mine. It will save us a little money, true, but manpower is the primary factor."

"Surely we can come to some arrangements?" Quark said, a bit of a desperate whine creeping into his voice. "I know this ship is perfect for your needs. How much would it take to persuade you to use my ship instead?"

Sisko tilted his head to the side. "Quark, is that a *bribe* you're offering me?"

"No, no," Quark said hastily, raising both hands. "What I meant is, how much of a *reduction* in price would it take for you to consider my ship instead of your friend's?"

Sisko gazed down at the baseball on his desk thoughtfully. "Forty bars of latinum?" he suggested.

"Done!" Quark cried. "I'll put through the invoice at once for two hundred and ten . . ." His voice trailed off.

Sisko was shaking his head. "Forty bars of latinum *total*," he said. "Not one bar more."

Quark let out a strangled cry. "You're killing me!"

"It's the best I can do," Sisko said. "And I'll wave the docking fees your ship has incurred while it's been here."

"I'll get back to you," Quark said. Muttering to himself, he stabbed the disconnect button. Sisko found himself staring at a blank screen, which was quickly replaced by the Federation logo of a starfield and two olive branches on a blue background.

"Let me guess," Dax said. "Right now he's finding out how much the hull is worth from salvage dealers."

"I expect so," Sisko said. "And thanks to Kira, we have a good idea what that is."

Kira was grinning. "Right, Captain," she said.

Half a minute later, Quark called again. "It's a

deal," he said to Sisko. He seemed more subdued than usual, Sisko thought, and almost sulky. Perhaps he was mourning the loss of two hundred and ten undeserved bars of gold-pressed latinum.

"Excellent," Sisko said. "If you'll put through your invoice, I'll see that it receives priority payment authorization."

"Thank you," Quark said sullenly, disconnecting.

Now, Sisko thought, to see about the wreck on the Bajoran moon. Then it would all be up to O'Brien and his people.

CHAPTER
5

FIVE O'CLOCK IN the morning is too early for delegates to arrive, Dr. Julian Bashir thought with a yawn as he strolled down the crossover bridge toward the docking ring. He hefted the DNA analyzer he was carrying. It only weighed fourteen kilos, but lugging it with him across half the station, he found it growing increasingly heavy. He'd have another look at the schematics later, he thought, and see if he could get the size trimmed down a little more.

At this hour, the station seemed oddly still, almost serene in its emptiness. None of the shops in the Promenade had opened for the day yet. Even Quark's bar was closed, and that, he reflected, spoke volumes about how dead the station became in the early hours of the morning. He'd only passed two other people so far, and one of them had been Dax out for her morning jog. She had waved and called a brief invitation for him to join her before passing by, but he'd declined. Her energy never ceased to amaze him.

Ahead, at the end of the crossover bridge, he spotted a knot of men and women blocking the passage. Something had to be going on here, he realized. Their low babble of voices grew steadily louder and more anxious. If someone was hurt, they'd need a doctor. Bashir quickened his pace to a near jog. But if someone was hurt, why hadn't he been called?

"Kill the Butcher of Belmast!" he suddenly heard a loud voice shouting.

"We want justice!" another cried.

"Bring him back to Bajor for trial!" a third voice called. "We know how to deal with Cardassians!"

Bashir groaned inwardly and drew up short. *Not again,* he thought. The crowd faced away from him, but now he recognized them all as Bajorans. The dangling earrings gave them away, if not their civilian clothes and anti-Cardassian sentiments. Somehow they'd found out that the Cardassian delegation had arrived, and they'd turned out in force as an unofficial harassment party. It seemed to happen every time a high-ranking Cardassian boarded the station.

But who was this "Butcher of Belmast" they were talking about? He frowned, trying to think back to where he'd heard of Belmast before. Wasn't it a remote province on Bajor? Hadn't some war atrocity been committed there? He shook his head. It wasn't his concern right now—he had delegates to screen for the peace conference. If he remembered, he'd ask Major Kira about it later.

Taking a deep breath, he started forward with determination. He'd never liked angry mobs, but he couldn't see any way around this one—they were completely blocking the walkway. To get around them, he'd have to retrace his steps to the Promenade and take a turbolift. Best to get it over with, he thought. Besides, they weren't mad at *him*.

The crowd seemed a little thinner to the left, so he eased his way between two women in pink and yellow robes. "Excuse me," he murmured. "I need through—station business."

"Aren't you Dr. Bashir?" one of the women asked. She was short and slightly overweight, with long reddish brown hair tied up behind her head, and her pale blue eyes held what looked like a fanatical gleam.

Bashir gulped and tried to remember if they had ever met before, but couldn't place her sharp features.

"Uh, yes," he admitted. "Do I know you?"

Instead of replying, she seized his arm and pulled him forward. "Let us through!" she called. "Let us through to Werron!"

Everyone around them turned to look, and Bashir found himself the center of attention. A little nervously, he forced a small nod and an even smaller wave. *What have I done to deserve this?* he wondered. He was almost certain he'd never met the Bajoran woman before. And who was Werron?

The crowd parted, and he rapidly found himself

pulled to the front. There, the Bajorans held placards in a variety of languages—English, Cardassian, and Bajoran. He scanned the ones he could read, and they all talked about "Justice" and "Cardassian War Criminals," as he'd half expected.

Six of Odo's men in tan and brown security uniforms held the line of Bajorans at bay. A couple of them gave Bashir welcoming nods, and the doctor felt a little better. They would rescue him if trouble started. Not that he really expected trouble. Relations remained good between humans and Bajorans at the moment, what with them applying for Federation membership and Captain Sisko being their Emissary and all.

"Vedek Werron," the woman said, "this is Julian Bashir, the station's medical officer."

A Vedek—no wonder they were so riled up. Bashir focused on the tall Bajoran wearing gray robes who turned at her voice. The man might dress simply, Bashir thought, but he carried himself like someone important. Vedeks were among the highest religious positions a Bajoran could attain, he knew, and their unique authority in Bajoran society allowed them to incite the masses with their words. Most of the trouble on DS9 between Bajorans and Cardassians could be traced to Bajoran religious leaders.

Vedek Werron had the thin, almost emaciated features of one who habitually fasted. His intense green eyes focused on Bashir, who felt instantly dissected by that gaze. *Like he can see into my soul,* Bashir thought with a shiver. Werron's short brown hair had been swept back over his scalp, and when he smiled, showing perfect white teeth, the image that leaped to Bashir's mind was that of a hungry tiger catching sight of breakfast.

"Doctor," Werron said in a low, powerful voice, stepping forward and taking Bashir's hand. He shook it in the human fashion. "I am delighted to make your acquaintance, sir. I have heard good things about you."

"And I am delighted to meet you, Vedek," Bashir said quickly. He extricated his hand as gently as he could; no sense offending the fellow. The sooner the niceties of introduction ended, the sooner he could get back to his work and away from here.

Vedek Werron searched Bashir's face. "It must be a great privilege serving with the Emissary," he said.

"Uh, yes, it is," Bashir said. Was this leading somewhere? He had a suspicion it was. "Captain Sisko is a fine commanding officer."

"I would like the chance to confer with him, but I'm afraid I haven't been able to reach him."

Bashir nodded. So that was it; Sisko didn't want to meet with Vedek Werron. Now Werron hoped to use him as an intermediary. Bashir felt a flash of triumph at having figured the man out.

But Werron merely said, "I am certain we'll be seeing more of each other, Doctor. It is, after all, a small universe." He motioned to his people, who drew back a half meter, leaving him a clear path. "I believe you were on a business call?" Again his smile reminded Bashir of a predator's.

"That's right," Bashir said. He swallowed and forced his eyes from Werron's face, feeling a cold knot form in his stomach. This was a dangerous man, something inside him said. He wished they hadn't met. And he certainly hoped they wouldn't meet again. Luckily business called.

Taking a deep breath, he ducked past Odo's deputies and continued toward the docking ports. He had to get to the Cardassians and administer his DNA test.

Behind him, he heard the Bajorans begin their chanting again: "Justice for Bajor . . . Justice for Bajor . . . Justice for Bajor . . ." Vedek Werron's deep, powerful voice boomed over the others, loud as a bell on a clear summer day.

When Bashir glanced back, he found Werron facing his own people, exhorting them to louder shouts of protest.

He forced his attention back to the task at hand. The Cardassian shuttle had parked at Docking Port 2. Odo stood just outside the open airlock door with two more deputies. Half a dozen Cardassians were standing just inside, out of sight of the Bajoran crowd, and they did not look happy.

"You're late, Doctor," Odo said gruffly.

"Sorry," he said. "I had a little trouble getting through the crowd."

Odo glanced back at them. "Yes, I can see how that might happen."

Bashir scanned the Cardassians' faces and was a trifle disappointed not to recognize anyone among them. The enemy you know and all that, he thought. Though their people might officially be at peace, he had seen little to end his distrust of Cardassians during his time on the station. If anything, he was more paranoid when dealing with them than ever. And he felt quite a bit of sympathy for the Bajorans— Cardassian occupation had nearly destroyed their world.

"I am Dr. Bashir," he said to the Cardassian at the front of the group, who seemed to be in charge. "I'm the station's chief medical officer."

"Gul Mekkar," the Cardassian replied. He was short and heavyset, with a lumpy, grayish face and thick corded neck. Mekkar folded his arms and glared. "We are here on a *peace* mission, Doctor. Why are we greeted by rioters, detained in our ship's airlock, and met by underlings instead of diplomats?"

Bashir wanted to roll his eyes and groan. It was going to be one of those days. "I'm sorry if we weren't prepared for you," he said, a trifle archly. "As you may recall, you arrived three hours early and wouldn't wait for proper clearance. Captain Sisko is in conference now and cannot be disturbed. He will join us as soon as he is able. In the meantime, *I* am here to ensure the safety and security of these proceedings. Anyone who plans to debark your ship will be required to undergo a DNA test to prove that they are in fact Cardassian."

Mekkar snorted. "Who else would we be— humans, perhaps? Or maybe Vulcans?"

Odo said, "As I already told you, we have reason to

believe changelings from the Gamma Quadrant may try to infiltrate these proceedings. This is a routine security measure, I assure you."

"Rubbish," Mekkar sneered. "It's another excuse for harassment, nothing more. No one mentioned tests when this conference was arranged."

Bashir said, "It's a surprise test, to make sure the changelings have no chance to prepare some way around it. The Valtusians have already submitted to the procedure, as has the entire command staff of DS9. It's fast and painless. I assure you, you won't feel the slightest discomfort."

Odo added, "You will not be allowed aboard the station until you and your entire crew submit to the screening process."

"This is an outrage!" Mekkar gestured angrily. "I—"

The Cardassian woman behind him leaned forward and whispered something in his ear. He listened for a second, then frowned.

"Very well," he said coldly to Bashir. "If it will allow us to get on with our work, you may proceed. But I warn you, if this is some sort of trick . . ." He let the threat hang between them.

One of those days, indeed. "And the rest of your people?" Bashir asked.

Many of the Cardassians behind Mekkar stirred, muttering to one another. None of them seemed happy with the idea of being tested.

Mekkar turned to his people. "They will submit as well," he said flatly. There were a few grumbles, but they quickly died down. Mekkar was not a Cardassian who was used to being argued with, Bashir saw.

At least it would be over soon. "Please place your hand on top," he said. He held out the DNA scanner.

Still glaring, Mekkar did so. The computer voice promptly announced that he was Cardassian.

"As you can see," he snarled, "I am who I say I am."

Bashir nodded and stepped back. "You may proceed."

Mekkar stomped out of the airlock, then turned and surveyed the mob cordoned off twenty meters away. His sneer grew, and Bashir heard him mutter, "Rabble!"

"That's him!" Bashir heard one of the Bajorans shout. "That's Mekkar!" Other voices cried, *"Cardassian Butcher!"* and *"Murderer!"*

Mekkar set his hands on his hips and glared at them. "On Cardassia," he announced in a loud voice, "this display would be punishable by death!"

More jeers came from the Bajorans.

Bashir sighed. He'd better get this over with quickly, he thought. The crowd was turning ugly. He only hoped Odo's people would be able to keep them in line.

The Cardassian woman who'd reasoned with Mekkar was next, and she placed her hand on the scanner before he asked. "Proceed," she said. There seemed to be a trace of amusement in her voice.

Bashir activated the scanner.

"What's your name?" he asked.

"Kloran." She brushed back her long, stringy black hair with one hand and gave him a brief smile. "I am Mekkar's second in these negotiations."

"Subject DNA passes," the computer said. "Subject is Cardassian." A wave of relief passed through Bashir. Every time he ran the scanner, he found he half expected someone to fail.

"You may proceed," he told her. "And thank you for your help."

"It was done in the interest of cooperation." She gave him a brief smile, then stepped forward and took Mekkar's arm. More jeers came from the Bajorans. Bashir glanced over and found Kloran smiling faintly, almost mockingly, at them, and a chill went through him. The two Cardassians made a rather daunting couple, he thought.

Chief Miles O'Brien felt beads of perspiration starting to form on his brow and shook his head. *Damn space suits.* He felt an overpowering urge to wipe his forehead, but there was no way he could reach inside through the faceplate. Next time they asked him what upgrades he wanted for DS9, he was going to ask for a spacedock.

For now, though, he'd just have to make do. Gritting his teeth, he raised his heavy cutting phaser, adjusting the controls to a tighter beam, and began burning through the final series of power couplings holding the *Galactic Queen*'s nacelles in place over the passenger compartment. Durasteel turned red, then white under the burst of energy, bubbling like one of Captain Sisko's gumbos. He could feel the heat even through the insulation in his gloves and space suit.

One power relay parted silently, then the second, then the third. Globules of rapidly cooling durasteel spiraled off into the darkness. O'Brien felt a drop of sweat run down the side of his face, then crawl along the line of his jaw. His faceplate began to fog up ever so slightly at the edges.

He shifted the phaser and fired again. Finally the fourth relay melted; the *Galactic Queen*'s starboard nacelle now floated freely in space. Only inertia held it in position.

O'Brien took a deep breath. The easy part was done. Clipping the phaser to his side, he took a second to glance down at his space suit's readouts. *Twenty degrees just isn't cold enough,* he thought. He'd set the controls as cold as they would go, but radiant heat from the phaser and the fused metal had raised the internal temperature of his space suit to nearly sixty degrees centigrade.

If only we had another couple of days, he thought. He hated working out in raw vacuum, but didn't see much choice. Fast and dirty, that was the only way to get the job done in time.

The durasteel had cooled back down. O'Brien turned his back to the ship, planted his feet against the hull, hooked his fingers under the power coupling he'd just severed, and heaved with all his strength. The ship had no weight in space; it was all a matter of getting its mass moving. Slowly, a fraction of a millimeter at a time, the nacelle parted from the main passenger compartment.

O'Brien let go after fifteen seconds. No sense straining any more against all that mass, he thought. Age was catching up to him; he didn't want Bashir doing an emergency procedure on his back to fix a slipped disc. He'd never hear the end of it.

He released the magnetic grips on his space boots and floated away from *Galactic Queen*'s hull, looking over his work with a critical eye. The port nacelle, already cut free, drifted a hundred meters away. He nodded to himself. Yes, it was coming along right on schedule.

"Chief," a tinny-sounding but recognizably female voice said through a burst of static. "We've got the dead hull."

He nudged the transmit bar with his chin. "Great," he said. He'd sent Ensign Polatta and her crew off in a runabout to fetch the *Progress* from the Bajoran moon. "How's she look?"

"Good, for scrap. Not so good for a starship."

"Bring her alongside the *Galactic Queen*. You'll have to round up the nacelles I just cut loose with tractor beams. We'll lick her into shape yet."

Starfleet's diplomatic team arrived just after midnight that night, and Sisko found himself standing outside the docking port, feeling bleary-eyed and tired.

Something hissed, and he felt a light touch on his arm. He jumped, a bit startled.

Dr. Bashir held up a hypo spray. "Vitamins," he said. "You're looking a little pale."

Leave it to Bashir to notice. "You, too, Doctor," he said.

"Yes, in my case it's lack of sleep." He stifled a yawn. "I've been up since four o'clock this morning."

"I've been meaning to thank you for covering the Cardassians' arrival for me."

"No problem," Bashir said. "Glad to help out. Actually, it was an interesting experience. I almost wish I could sit in on the negotiations just to see how everyone interacts."

"I'm expecting fireworks," Sisko admitted. Federation, Maquis, Valtusian, and Cardassian diplomats struck him as about the least compatible bunch imaginable. Even the Klingons and the Romulans could be more reasonable than Cardassians.

The door rolled aside, and a strikingly beautiful Vulcan woman walked out, looking around curiously. Her short black hair and pointed, almost elfin ears loaned her delicately boned face an almost ethereal quality. Sisko found his gaze moving from her face to the stunning aqua dress she wore off one shoulder. Matching blue sandals, studded with gemstones, completed the outfit.

"You must be Captain Sisko," she said, her voice flat and emotionless.

"That's right," he said. "And you are . . .?"

"Ambassador T'Pao." She turned and indicated the heavyset man with short reddish blond hair following her. "This is Ambassador DuQuesne, and behind him is Ambassador Strockman." Strockman, thin to the point of emaciation, with pinched cheeks and thinning black hair cropped close to his skull, gave a curt nod.

Sisko smiled politely, then did the introductions.

"We have designed a test to check for changeling infiltration," he said. "It only takes a minute and is completely painless."

He half expected a series of protests, but T'Pao merely nodded once. "Proceed."

"Doctor?" Sisko said.

Bashir stepped forward. "If you would place your hand on the scanner," he said.

T'Pao did so, and it promptly announced that she was Vulcan. Then DuQuesne stepped forward and placed his hand on top.

"A good idea," T'Pao commented. "One cannot be too careful in negotiations such as these."

"Our thoughts exactly," Sisko said. He couldn't help but grin. At least the Federation ambassadors understood the necessity of security.

Both DuQuesne and Strockman passed the DNA test.

"Now," T'Pao said, "if you could show us to our quarters. It has been a long trip, and I believe my colleagues require rest. They have become somewhat . . . irritable."

"Of course." Sisko turned and led the way toward the turbolift. "Your suites are on the habitat ring . . ." he began.

"Sir," Ensign McCormick said. "I *think* I'm picking up a ship on the extreme limits of sensor range."

A new ship? Dax crossed to the ensign's console and studied the readouts over his shoulder. The only ship she was still expecting belonged to the Maquis delegates to the peace conference, and if she knew her Maquis, they'd be playing it very cautiously. After all, DS9 was a Federation outpost, and technically they would fall under Federation law the moment they set foot aboard. Despite all of the assurances Starfleet and the Valtusians had given them, they must still be a little paranoid. She didn't blame them.

On the other hand, it could be a Dominion ship looking them over from the distance. . . .

Dax reached down, channeled extra power to the sensor relays, and scanned the ship again.

"Bingo," she said, as the results came up on the ensign's monitor screen. It was an old Federation transport ship, probably decommissioned and sold off to colonists years ago. The station's computer identified it as the *Uganda*.

"Sir? Bingo?" The ensign gazed at her blankly.

They were getting younger every year, Dax thought.

"An old Earth expression," she explained. "It means 'you're right.' "

"Are they . . . Jem'Hadar?"

"Wrong direction." She moved aside so McCormick could see the readouts. "Take a look at that. It's a Federation ship. Or used to be."

"Maquis . . ." the ensign breathed.

Dax smiled. "A pretty good guess, especially since we're expecting them." She returned to the science station. "I'll take it from here."

"Yes, sir."

Dax hailed the ship. "This is Lieutenant Commander Jadzia Dax of *Deep Space Nine*. Maquis ship, please identify yourself."

There was no response. Probably still looking us over, she thought, and who could blame them? It must have taken a lot on the Valtusians' part to even get them this far.

"Maquis ship," she said again, "please identify yourself."

"This is the *Uganda*," a male voice responded hesitantly a moment later. It was an audio-only signal. How paranoid were these people? "We are here for the peace conference."

"You're early," she said. "Our docking schedule is full for the next three hours. If you'd care to wait, I'll fit you in—"

"We've just picked up a Federation warship approaching at high warp!" The pitch of his voice rose half an octave. "You've betrayed us—"

"Not true," Dax said. Damn, what a time for a Federation ship to show up! "Hold your position, *Uganda*. You have nothing to worry about."

She punched the new ship up on her console—the

Excalibur, with high-priority clearance. She groaned inwardly. This was *really* going to screw up her docking schedule. Perhaps they'd beam people over instead of docking . . .

She split the screen to monitor both ships at once. The Maquis vessel had already come about and begun accelerating away from DS9. She saw that its warp coil was powering up.

"Uganda," she said, "the Federation ship is only here to drop off delegates for the conference. It will depart as soon as it's done. You have nothing to worry about."

"I have your word on that, Commander?"

"That's right."

"We will withdraw for now," his voice said. "We'll return in three hours. *Uganda* out."

"DS9 out," Dax said. She nodded. No doubt about it, they were nervous. At least they were coming back, though. Hopefully the *Excalibur* would be gone by then.

CHAPTER
6

SISKO WATCHED THE colorful flicker of lights in the Ops's two-person transporter chamber as a figure began to materialize. The *Excalibur* had come to a stationary position between DS9 and the wormhole, and now Lieutenant Colfax was in the process of beaming aboard.

The hum of the transporter faded away as Colfax materialized. He carried what appeared to be a cloth satchel in one hand. It seemed quite heavy, Sisko noted. Stepping down from the transporter, Colfax smiled coolly and offered his hand to Sisko.

Sisko shook it. "Won't you come into my office," he said.

"Certainly," Colfax said, shifting the satchel to his other hand and following.

"We weren't expecting you so soon," Sisko said

over his shoulder. "Admiral Dulev said thirty-two hours."

"We made excellent time," Colfax said. "I had the *Excalibur*'s captain shave every second off the run that she could. You know how important speed is here. I'm sorry to have held up your away team this long, but I believe you'll find it necessary."

"The admiral didn't say much about it."

He nodded. "We're taking every precaution possible, in case the changelings are monitoring our subspace communications. Now, I'd appreciate it if you'd call in your away team. I want to brief them as quickly as possible."

"Certainly." He paused in the doorway to his office. "Dax?"

"I'll get them here," she called.

"Thanks." Sisko entered his office, then closed the door behind them. To Colfax he said, "Can I offer you a drink?"

"No, thank you," Colfax said. He set his satchel on a chair, then ran his finger along the seam and peeled it open. "I'm afraid this is only a brief stopover for me. I'm here to drop off equipment for your away team, that's all. I trust they're ready to leave?"

"Their ship is waiting," Sisko said. That was close enough to true; it would be a matter of hours now before the last tests were complete. He perched on the edge of his desk and folded his arms.

"Good," Colfax said.

The door chirped. "Come," Sisko said.

Kira, Odo, and Worf filed in. "You wanted to see us, sir?" Worf asked, his voice low and gravely.

Sisko indicated his guest. "This is Lieutenant Colfax from Admiral Dulev's office. Apparently he has additional equipment for you."

"That's right," Dulev said. He pulled a thick metallic belt from the satchel and turned around to face them. "This is an experimental device which the Romulans have loaned us specifically for this mission. It's called a personal cloaker."

A personal cloaker? Sisko found himself leaning forward to study the belt. Surely it couldn't be a cloaking device; it was far too small. He frowned a bit, studying a series of silver boxes connected with mesh links. It had a small control panel on the front, he noted, which appeared to consist of a simple power readout and an on/off switch.

Odo asked, "What exactly does it do?"

"I'm getting to that." Colfax snapped the belt around his waist and looked up. "As the name suggests, it's a variant on the cloaking devices which conceal Romulan ships in space. It creates a distortion wave which surrounds your body, rendering you effectively invisible to the naked eye. Watch."

Colfax activated one of the buttons on the belt's control panel. The air around him rippled for a second, and then he faded from view.

Sisko stood bolt upright, shocked. The security implications were devastating. With one of these, someone could walk into the most closely guarded Federation installation undetected.

A second later Colfax reappeared. "Simple, yes?" he said.

"How many of these things are there?" Odo demanded.

"I've brought two for use in your mission," Colfax said. "The third one must remain with me. Our people are working with Romulan scientists to perfect the devices. They may well offer our first counter to the advantages offered by the changelings' morphing abilities."

"How do they work?" Sisko asked.

"Simplicity itself," Colfax said. He removed the belt and laid it flat on the desk so everyone could see the control panel on the front. "There is an on/off button and a time readout."

"A time readout?" Worf asked, frowning.

Colfax hesitated. "There are problems with the personal cloakers," he admitted. "They use a fantastic amount of energy. Our most powerful battery can only run one for eight minutes."

Odo seemed to relax a little, Sisko saw, and he knew why: With only eight minutes of power, it would be difficult for anyone to use them effectively for sabotage.

"I know it's not a lot of time," Colfax said, "but it's one extra advantage you didn't have before. It could well mean the difference between getting caught and eluding capture."

"There is almost something cowardly about hiding behind invisible shields," Worf said, a little stiffly.

"Commander Worf," Colfax said, rising and facing

him, "the entire Alpha Quadrant risks subjugation under the changelings. We will not allow this to happen—whatever the cost. Honor is one of our least valuable commodities right now. Is that understood?"

Worf bristled a little, but nodded. Sisko could tell it troubled him nonetheless.

"Good," Colfax said. He drew two more belts from his satchel and handed one to Kira and one to Worf. "Wear them under your clothes at all times on this mission," he said. "I know they're bulky, but they're the best we can do. And one more thing: If you're in danger of being caught, or if you exhaust the belts' power supplies, destroy them. They cannot be allowed to fall into the enemy's hands." He put the belt he'd used for his demonstration away. "Any questions?"

A little to his surprise, Sisko found he didn't have any, and neither did anyone else. The personal cloakers seemed straight-forward enough.

"Good." Colfax smiled and sealed up his satchel. "I wish you all luck and all success. And now, Captain," he said to Sisko, "I've got to get back to my ship."

Sisko rose. "I'll walk you out," he said.

CHAPTER
7

TWO HOURS LATER, Kira found herself standing next to Worf on the transporter pad in Ops.

"Energize," O'Brien said.

Kira tensed a little as the two of them beamed over to the *Progress*. She didn't know what to expect, but she had a feeling in the pit of her stomach that she wouldn't like it.

The second she materialized, she sniffed the air as discreetly as she could, but tasted none of the *Galactic Queen's* foul odor. That was one mark in this ship's favor, she thought, glancing around. Beside her, Worf was doing likewise.

The *Progress* had a large oval cabin, with seats for a pilot and copilot in the front, facing a broad viewport. The middle section of the ship had fifteen rows of seats that could recline into beds. Behind them, half screened off by panels, stood the warp engines and life-support panels. The only thing lacking seemed to be a transporter. Hopefully they wouldn't need one.

Right now DS9 hung before them, visible through the forward viewport, spinning ever so slowly. There were starships attached to every single port on the docking ring, Kira noted, and to two of the three tall docking pylons jutting over the station. She hadn't seen the station this busy since the Bajor's rogue moon had passed by several years before. Tourists and sightseers had flocked aboard to see the spectacle.

Chief O'Brien and Odo materialized a few meters away in a shimmer of light. She forced her attention from DS9 and walked back to join them.

"All systems check out, Major," O'Brien said with a broad grin. "She's ready to go. Maximum warp six-point-two, with a maximum safe range of about two hundred and fifty light-years."

"You're sure the nacelles won't fall off?" she said.

"Major . . ." His crestfallen expression betrayed his disappointment in her lack of faith.

"Okay, okay," she said, laughing a little. "I'm sure everything's fine. But I'll run my own diagnostics, if you don't mind."

"I'd be disappointed if you didn't," he said.

Kira returned to the pilot's seat and brought the diagnostic tests online. Quickly she ran them through their paces and found that O'Brien hadn't exaggerated—everything did indeed check out at a hundred percent. There wasn't so much as an uneven flicker in the power couplings.

"You're a miracle worker," she said. "I never would have believed it."

He blushed a little. "Well, I had help," he said. "I put eight people on it."

Kira began to nod. It would do. For the first time, she thought this mad plan might actually work. And with the Romulan personal cloakers . . .

"Any questions?" O'Brien asked.

"None," Kira said. "We'll leave in half an hour. Just give us time to change into civilian clothes and we'll be set."

"Great. I have one more thing to show you all first, though," he said. "If you'll follow me?" Turning, he headed aft.

She accompanied him to the screened off engine area. There, he paused by the back wall.

"This is it," he said, indicating battered, stained durasteel panels.

"What?" Worf said, wandering closer. "A wall?"

"No, I see the seams," Odo said, moving forward and looking closely. "Very ingenious, Chief."

Worf stepped forward and ran his hands over the panels. "I see nothing," he said.

Kira too peered closely at it, but couldn't see much more than durasteel plating. "Are you sure?" she said to Odo.

O'Brien was grinning. "It takes a pro to spot it," he said.

Odo snorted. "Or someone who's been watching Quark too long," he said.

O'Brien stepped forward, pushed in a hidden catch, then slid the panel to one side, revealing a compartment large enough to hide a person.

"In case of trouble," he said, "I put in two secret compartments. You can hide in them. They're fully screened, so if someone scans the ship, they won't pick up life signs."

"Aren't you forgetting Odo?" Kira said.

"It's hard for a scanner to pick up a changeling at the best of times," Odo said. "If I turn myself into something inanimate, they won't spot me, either."

She nodded. O'Brien seemed to have thought of everything. Again she felt a surge of optimism. This mission really could succeed, she told herself.

"Then let's move," she said. "The sooner we get going, the sooner we get back." She tapped her badge. "Major Kira to DS9. Four to beam over."

Odo beamed back to DS9 with the others, but while Kira and Worf went to change into civilian clothes, he returned to his office. All the security details for the peace conference had already been set, but he wanted to take a last look at them. This would be the first major event on the station that he'd missed in all his years as head of security, and he didn't want anything to happen while he was gone. Nobody was indispensable, of course, but he liked feeling needed. Since he'd rejected his own kind, it gave him a measure of comfort knowing there was a place he would always be welcome. He wouldn't allow anything to jeopardize that. He wanted a home to return to when this mission ended.

His door opened, and Captain Sisko stepped in with a large square box in his hands.

Odo rose. "Captain," he said. "What brings you here?"

"This," Sisko said, indicating the box. Odo looked it over, but it appeared innocuous.

"A bomb?" he asked.

"A peace initiative," Sisko said. "It contains a holographic recording inviting the Founders to a peace conference. If you're caught in the Gamma Quadrant, it might buy you some extra time. At the very least it gives you a legitimate excuse to be there." He smiled a little too thinly, Odo thought. "And, of course, there *is* always the chance your people will choose to take me up on the offer . . . remote as it seems now."

"Very remote," Odo said dryly. He couldn't imagine anything more surprising when it came to the changelings; they had stated their intention of conquering the Alpha Quadrant quite clearly. "But I will, of course, pass it on . . . should the opportunity arise."

"That's all I ask." Sisko set the box on the edge of Odo's desk, then turned toward the door. Almost as an afterthought, he added, "Take care of them, Odo. I want my people back alive. And that includes you."

"Of course," Odo said, straightening a little. Sisko

was depending on him. Sisko needed him. "I'll do my best."

Kira studied her reflection in the full-length mirror next to her closet: a dark blue one-piece suit, with a stripe of silver across the left shoulder and a splash of gold at the wrists. The sleeves flared a little more widely than she liked, allowing two silver bracelets to show, but she could live with that. What she missed was her earring; the right side of her head looked odd without it, and she felt a little off-balance. Imagination of course, since the earring didn't weigh much, but still, it didn't look or feel like *her*, like Major Kira Nerys the Bajoran, without it.

She turned to the side and studied her profile. She looked *very* different, she decided. Nobody on Bajor would recognize her now. Not even—

A loud series of electronic beeps interrupted her thoughts. "Come in," she called.

The door whisked open. Captain Sisko stepped in and did a double take.

"What do you think?" Kira asked, turning around once for him.

"You look quite different, Major," he said.

"Good different or bad different?" she asked with a wicked grin. She'd see if he'd fall into that trap.

"Like a Gamma Quadrant native," he said with a laugh. "The Maquis ship will be here soon, and I wanted to wish you luck before you go."

"Thank you," she said seriously.

"Is there anything else you want to bring with

you?" he asked. "Any tools or weapons or . . . anything?"

Kira indicated her pack, which sat on the table by the door. It held everything from emergency food rations to high-tensor cord to extra power packs for their phasers. "Worf and I already went through that," she said. "I think we're set for anything we come across." *I hope,* she mentally added.

"Take care of yourself, Major," he said somberly. "I'm counting on you to bring everyone else back alive."

Kira swallowed. "Yes, sir," she said, and she felt a sudden flush of pride. He was counting on her. She knew she couldn't let him down.

Then he nodded once and left.

She'd do her best to make sure she lived up to his expectations. She glanced at the mirror one last time, picked up her pack, and headed for the transporter in Ops. Time to get going. The sooner they left, the sooner they'd be back.

Worf shouldered his pack and started for the door. This was just a mission like any other, he told himself. They would go, get the informant and his data, and come back. Never mind that he had to dress in a loose-fitting gray tunic, with a hood that could be pulled up to cover his head; the importance of the mission far outweighed his own comfort and fashion sense. But he'd still take a good uniform any day.

As his door opened, he stopped short. Captain Sisko stood outside, poised to knock.

"Captain," he said, stepping back. "Won't you . . . come in?"

"Thank you, Commander," Sisko said, stepping forward. "I've only known you a short while," he said as the door closed behind him, "but I've developed a deep respect for your talents."

Worf felt his chest puff out a little. "Thank you, sir," he said. Sisko was not a human given to extravagant praise, he knew, and coming from him, this meant a lot.

"Although Major Kira is in charge of this mission, you're still the ranking Starfleet officer. I wanted you to know that I'm counting on you to make sure our interests are fully protected."

Worf nodded. That much went without saying. He intended to give one hundred percent of his energy and attention to making sure they succeeded.

"And . . ." Sisko went on. "Good luck. Bring everyone back alive, Worf."

"Thank you, sir," Worf said. He'd do his best. Even if it killed him.

Sisko accompanied Worf to Ops, then watched as Dax beamed first the Klingon and Kira, then Odo over to the *Progress* using the two-man transporter.

He had nodded to each of them, and he saw how each took it personally to heart. Pep talks had never come easily to him, but this time he'd meant every word. He was depending on them to make it back. Succeed or fail, he wanted them home safely.

Dax joined him and leaned on his shoulder. "You

have the gloomiest expression on your face that I've ever seen," she said. "They'll be back. Let them do their jobs while you do yours. Come on, I'll buy you a drink at Quark's. I hear O'Brien and Bashir are planning another rematch in their ongoing darts tournament."

"Maybe later, old man."

"It's a date. I'll collect you at six."

He gazed over at one of the monitors, which showed the *Progress* slowly accelerating away from the station. Suddenly the wormhole opened before the ship like a dazzling blue whirlpool in space—and just as suddenly it was gone, the *Progress* along with it.

"Stay well, my friends," he murmured. "Stay well."

CHAPTER
8

AN HOUR LATER, the door to his office beeped. Sisko sighed and looked up from his computer terminal. Just as he was starting to get a handle on this week's reports . . . just as he was starting to forget that he'd just sent three of his people on what might turn out to be a suicide mission by burying himself in routine work . . . reality had to intrude.

"Come," he called.

Dax stuck her head in the office, and Sisko relaxed a little. It was hard to be annoyed by your best friend. "Yes, Dax?" he said.

"I thought you'd want to know, Benjamin," she said. "The Maquis ship just docked."

"Thank you," he said, tabbing off the screen and rising. "Have you told Dr. Bashir yet?"

"I've already alerted him." Dax matched his stride

as Sisko headed for the turbolift. "He's going to meet us there."

"Us?" Sisko shot her a puzzled glance. She hadn't expressed any interest in meeting the other delegates; she had to have an ulterior motive. He knew her symbiont well enough to realize that.

She smiled. "Well, they were a little nervous about coming here. This *is* a Federation base, and when the *Excalibur* showed up, it really spooked them. I gave them my word that this wasn't a trap, so I thought I'd be there to make sure everything goes smoothly."

That was more like it. But something still seemed to be bothering her. As the lift doors shut, he asked, "Is something else concerning you?"

"Well, yes, now that you mention it," she said. "Benjamin, you've looked better, and you seem distracted. Is there anything I can do to help?"

Sisko forced a smile. "I'm just feeling a little overwhelmed. There's too much going on at once."

"You mean between the mission to the Gamma Quadrant and the peace conference."

Those, and a thousand other things, Sisko thought. He nodded.

"Don't worry about Kira and Worf. You know they have a good chance to make it out," Dax said. "Those personal cloakers are enough to get them out of anything. And Odo *is* a Founder. The Jem'Hadar practically fall to the floor and worship him whenever they see him."

Sisko nodded. "Yes, but I can't help but feel I should have gone myself."

"They volunteered."

"I know—and I know my accompanying them wouldn't have helped."

"And you *are* needed at this peace summit," Dax went on. "Put your energies where they'll do the most good."

"Like here," Sisko said with a quick grin. Somehow, she always knew what to say to him. Sometimes he thought she knew him better than he knew himself.

"Like here," she said firmly.

"Dax, sometimes I think you should have been a psychiatrist."

She made a face. "That's so *boring.*"

The doors opened. Sisko pulled his dress uniform a trifle straighter. "Let's get it over with," he said.

Philip Twofeathers sucked in a deep breath and tried to hide his growing nervousness. His wide, flat face with its prominent nose, dark eyes, and deep reddish brown skin told of his Native American heritage more than his conservative gray one-piece suit, and for an instant he almost wished he'd worn something more comfortable. His people—descendants of the Cherokee—had settled a frontier planet called Dorvanto twenty years previously, and they had gone back to their people's old ways. He would have felt more comfortable in a leather vest, breechcloth, and moccasins. It had been many years since he'd worn such confining clothing. Unlike the Starfleet vessels, Maquis ships had no stuffy dress codes.

Why they had selected him, he still didn't quite understand. They had said it was because of his honesty, his dedication, and his commitment. Every other member of the Maquis felt the same way, though, he knew. They wouldn't be fighting an impossible guerrilla war against an overwhelmingly superior opponent like Cardassia if they didn't.

He glanced over at Myriam Kravitz beside him. She, too, was from the Maquis, but it was her three years of legal training at Starfleet Academy—she left to join the Maquis when the Federation ceded her Homeworld, too, to Cardassia in a peace treaty—that bought her a place at the negotiating table.

The airlocks slowly matched pressure between their ship and *Deep Space Nine,* and then their hatch opened. Twofeathers saw a gigantic blood-red cog slowly roll to one side. It was the space station's hatch, he realized suddenly, disconcerted.

"You first," Myriam whispered.

He nodded reassuringly to her, keeping his face impassive, then proceeded down the short passage and out into the docking ring. There were three humanoids waiting to greet them: one tall, imposing-looking black man in a command uniform, with his head shaved and a short beard; a Trill woman, her straight black hair tied behind her head, revealing the patterning of her spots on her forehead and neck; and another human, this one with short wavy black hair.

"Philip Twofeathers?" the Trill asked.

"Yes," he said, his voice deep and booming.

"I am Lieutenant Commander Dax," she said. "We spoke earlier."

"Yes," he said.

"I am Captain Sisko," the black man said, nodding politely. "This is Dr. Bashir. On behalf of the Federation, I would like to welcome you aboard DS9, Ambassadors."

"Thank you," Twofeathers said. "This is my associate, Myriam Kravitz."

"Pleased to make your acquaintance, Captain Sisko," she said.

He nodded to her. "We have one security test before we admit you to the station," he went on. "A DNA test to verify that you are, indeed, who you say you are."

"My DNA patterns are not on file with Starfleet," Twofeathers said. Was this some kind of trick? He didn't like the sound of it.

"It's to make sure you're human and not changelings trying to infiltrate the peace process," Bashir said quickly. "Anything which brings stability to this quadrant is against their best interests."

"But what else can you do with my DNA once you have it?" Twofeathers said. He shook his head. No, this would not do at all. "This is against all diplomatic protocols as I understand them. I refuse."

"Then," Sisko said, "you can get right back on your ship. Go back to the Maquis. Tell them that you single-handedly derailed the entire peace process because you didn't want to prove to us that you are human."

"We don't do anything with the DNA except scan it to make sure you're human," Bashir said.

"Use a tricorder."

"The changelings can fool even a tricorder," he said.

Twofeathers snorted. Paranoid fools.

Kravits stepped forward. "My DNA is already on file with Starfleet," she said. "Test me."

Bashir held out the box he was holding. "Place your hand on top," he said. "It's painless. You won't feel a thing."

Twofeathers watched, feeling his heart start to beat a little faster with concern, as Myriam did what she was told.

"Scanning," the box said. "Subject DNA passes. Subject is human."

Myriam stepped back, flexing her fingers and staring at her hand. The breath caught in Twofeathers's throat—was she all right?

Suddenly she looked at him and nodded. "Do it," she said. "I don't see any harm."

The Federation officers looked relieved. Twofeathers studied them a second, then nodded his assent. They had DNA on file from many members of the Maquis, he thought, and it had done them little good in the past. He didn't see how it could hurt now, either.

"Very well," he said and stretched out his hand. A second later the box announced that he, too, was human.

"This way," Sisko said. "Perhaps you'd like a tour of the station before we show you to your quarters?"

"Yes," Twofeathers said. "I have heard of a place here called . . . Quark's? . . . which a number of friends recommend."

Sisko blanched a bit at that. "Quark's," he said, sounding completely nonplussed.

Twofeathers folded his arms, tilted back his head, and stared impassively up at him. "Quark's," he repeated.

Lieutenant Dax smiled. "Why don't you let me show them around," she suggested to Sisko.

"Very well," he said. He smiled briefly at Twofeathers and Kravitz. "I leave you in Dax's capable hands." As he turned to go, Twofeathers overheard him whisper, "Just keep them out of *trouble*, okay, old man?"

Old man? Twofeathers frowned in bewilderment. What kind of nickname was that for a woman?

But Dax merely smiled and hooked her arms through theirs, leading them toward the turbolift. "One of the station's many attractions is Quark's Place," she said. "Julian here is an excellent darts player—do you know the game?—and I believe he's going to be in a tournament tonight."

"Darts," Twofeathers said. It was a game he'd always enjoyed as a boy, though he preferred throwing knives these days. "Aren't those similar to tiny arrows?" he said, trying to sound naive.

"Very similar, actually," Dr. Bashir said from behind him. "I'd be glad to give you some pointers, if you'd like."

"I think I would," Twofeathers said. A tournament might be a good way to make a little money, he thought. He smiled inwardly. It was rather amusing, actually, that Federation losses would go straight into the Maquis war fund.

But he couldn't let himself forget the other reason he'd come. There was a lot of war surplus available on Bajor . . . arms and equipment the Maquis desperately needed if they were going to win the fight with Cardassia. Peace negotiations were fine, but knowing the Cardassians and the Federation, he had little hope of success. So while he could operate here in the open, he intended to take advantage of his every opportunity. Rumor said that Quark could get anything you wanted, for a price. . . .

CHAPTER
9

AFTER A BUMPY ride through the wormhole, Kira brought the *Progress* into the Gamma Quadrant. Instantly she ran a long-range scan . . . and picked up nothing. Not a sign of a ship, Jem'Hadar or otherwise. That had always amazed her. If this were her quadrant, she would have put some kind of watchers here to monitor traffic through the wormhole. But then, if the changelings had a weakness, it had to be their cocky attitude. They felt they were born to rule the universe. Present company excluded, of course.

"We're safe," she said. "No sign of Jem'Hadar ships."

"Excellent," Worf said from behind her.

Kira punched in the coordinates and set the autopilot. The ship accelerated smoothly on a new bearing . . . the Daborat system, fifty-seven light-years distant.

"Since there's no sign of trouble," Odo said, "I'll leave you to your piloting."

"We'll call you if anything comes up," Kira promised.

When she glanced back, she saw Odo transforming into a shining golden glob. He oozed across the floor, then one end arched up and fountained into a bucket sitting on top of one of the padded seats in the passenger section. She didn't know how he managed to fit all of himself into such a small space, but somehow he did.

"I would never be able to get used to that," Worf said, dropping into the copilot's seat beside her. "It looks so—*confining.*"

She swiveled around to face him. His knobby forehead was furrowed as he stared back toward Odo.

"I'm sure he finds it safe and comfortable."

Worf grunted, then turned around to look at her.

"Since we're going to be flying for most of the day," she said, "this seems like a good chance to get to know one another better. Tell me about yourself, Commander. What's it like being the first Klingon in Starfleet?"

Worf sighed and rolled his eyes. "That is the question everyone in the universe seems to ask," he said.

"And you're sick of it."

He nodded.

"I understand. I can't tell you how many times I've

been asked by Bajorans what it's like to serve under a Federation captain."

"Oh?"

Kira thought she saw a spark of interest in his eyes. Perhaps that was the key to winning his friendship, she thought—finding common ground. But wasn't that the case with all sentient life-forms throughout the galaxy? *Every life-form except Ferengi,* she thought. They didn't have friends. They had customers.

She shrugged. "It's a living."

"A living . . . I will remember that answer," Worf said. He seemed to relax a bit.

"I was raised by human parents," Worf said, "so I grew up with Starfleet. Had my Klingon parents lived, I would never have joined." He jerked his chin back the way they had come. "I would probably be with my brothers now, helping to seize Cardassian territory."

"You don't sound thrilled with that idea."

"It is a living."

Kira did a double take. Was that a sense of humor?

"I always used to think I'd make a great farmer," she said. "As a child, I dreamed of running through the fields, smelling the sun-ripened plants, feeling the sun on my back and the soil between my toes. I sometimes wonder if that's what I'd be doing today, if it weren't for the Cardassian occupation. I might be a mother with four or five children, running my farm, living off the land . . ."

"I cannot picture you as a mother," Worf said. "Or as a farmer."

Kira sighed. "It's hard, but a part of me still wants it."

Then Worf began to tell her of life on the *Enterprise* before its destruction, of his son Alexander and his friends Data and Geordi LaForge and Deanna Troi and she found herself actually enjoying his company. Secretly she had been half dreading the long flight with him. Now it seemed it might be more pleasant than she would have thought possible.

Four hours later, as Worf and Kira were comparing their encounters with the life-form named Q, alarms began to ring. Instantly Kira swiveled her seat around and disengaged the autopilot.

Worf said, "We're being scanned. There's a vessel approaching quickly from behind."

"I see it," Kira muttered. Then she looked up. "It's not on an intercept course. And they're no longer scanning us." She reached over and switched off the alarm. Silence flooded through the cabin. Kira found her heart racing. She took a deep breath to calm herself. It sounded like a gulp.

"We do not have weapon systems aboard," Worf pointed out. "Perhaps we did not register as a threat."

"Or perhaps they're smugglers watching out for Jem'Hadar patrols," Kira said. She continued to watch the ship on the monitor until it left scanner range. Only then did she return control of the *Progress* to the autopilot.

It was going to be a long trip, she realized.

CHAPTER
10

QUARK'S BAR WAS packed. Jammed toe to claw to wing, O'Brien thought a little gloomily as he surveyed the hundreds of beings massed around the bar, crowding the gambling tables, and generally mobbing the place. He was wedged in at the end of the bar between a pair of Bajorans who were noisily arguing about some aspect of the Cardassian occupation and a grizzled old Taltic whose iridescent blue-green scales stank from too many months locked aboard a starship. You could always tell a Harden space traveller spacer by his odor, O'Brien thought. Half the tramp freighters working this sector seemed to make DS9 a port of call these days, and he would have bet that not one of them carried proper bathing facilities anywhere aboard. The Taltic, nursing a bottle of Qualian sea-brandy, was typical. And he didn't seem to be going anywhere soon. In fact, the only place that *wasn't* packed was the dartboard area at the back, stuck under the walkway to the holosuites.

O'Brien sucked in an angry breath as one of the Bajorans accidentally jostled him, almost spilling his mug of Tirellian stout. Bloody hell, would Bashir never show up? Had the doctor completely forgotten their dart game?

Taking another sip of the stout, he winced and tried to catch Quark's eye. The stuff was vile, no doubt about it, and he regretted letting Quark talk him into trying it. Good old-fashioned lager, that's what he was in the mood for tonight. "That and a dart game," he muttered to himself.

Quark was too busy piling orders onto Rom's tray to notice O'Brien. Now that Nog was off at Starfleet Academy, Quark seemed to be perpetually short-handed, O'Brien thought, and the Ferengi was just too cheap to hire another waiter. O'Brien took another sip of the stout. It had a certain afterkick, he decided, which wasn't half bad. He could get used to it.

The Bajorans jostled him again, this time spilling half his stout across the bar.

"Watch it," he said sharply.

The Bajoran glanced back at him. "You talking to me, human?" he demanded.

"That's right," O'Brien said, standing to face him. "You knocked my drink over."

"Maybe you shouldn't sit on top of me," the Bajoran countered rudely. "Maybe you owe *me* an apology, Earther."

O'Brien sucked in an angry breath. "I'll have you know," he began hotly.

Suddenly Quark was there, patting his arm soothingly. "Easy there, Chief," he said, leaning forward to refill O'Brien's mug from a pitcher. "I can't afford any more murder investigations this month. It cost me a fortune paying off the families of the two Caxtonians you killed in that brawl last week."

O'Brien blinked in puzzlement. Caxtonians were huge, hairy humanoids with great natural piloting skills but few social graces. He knew better than tackling one in a fight. He'd certainly never killed a pair of them in a brawl.

"Two . . . *Caxtonians?*" the Bajoran said.

Quark nodded seriously and lowered his voice to a conspiratorial whisper. "Oh, yes, O'Brien here, he's an expert in Klingon martial arts. You should have seen it. Ten seconds after he waded into the fight, he'd decapitated one and shattered the other's skull with a flying kick." He shook his head. "I've never seen anything like it."

Catching on, O'Brien bared his teeth and snarled a bit, the way he'd once seen Worf do it when Quark had pissed him off.

The Bajoran paled. "My apologies for spilling your drink," he said quickly. "Put it on my tab," he told Quark. Then he quickly gathered up his own glass and hurried off toward the gambling tables with his friend.

"Thanks," O'Brien said, leaning on the bar, "but I can take care of myself, Quark."

"Nothing to do with you," Quark said, setting up a

new batch of glasses. "They were too busy arguing to drink. I was just clearing space for paying customers."

A pair of long-necked Igrids, tall and graceful, almost birdlike creatures covered in blue feathers, but with six tentacles instead of arms, quickly took the vacant seats. Quark gave them a hideously toothy but sincere-seeming smile.

"What can I get you ladies?" he asked.

Ladies? O'Brien thought. How could he tell?

The two Igrids tittered drunkenly, tentacles slapping on the bar's counter.

"Mooth!" one said.

"Make mine a double!" said the other.

"Mine, too!" said the first.

"Coming right up," Quark said, and he began mixing a fluorescent green concoction in a pitcher for them.

"Let me know if Julian shows up," O'Brien said, sliding off his stool. "I'll be practicing."

"You got it," Quark said.

O'Brien headed for the dartboard, weaving his way between tables. As he went, he became conscious of the fact that quite a few Bajorans had grown silent and were staring at him. He swallowed a little nervously, not liking the attention.

"He killed five Klingons bare-handed last week!" he overheard one saying to another. *"Five!"*

It seemed the rumor mill had started spreading Quark's tale. O'Brien shook his head. All he wanted was a quiet game of darts. He didn't want a reputation as some kind of Captain Kirk.

"Chief!" he heard a familiar voice shout.

Glancing toward the door, he spotted Bashir there along with Dax and a pair of humans he didn't know. He grinned and waved toward the dartboard, and Bashir gave him the "okay" sign. Now O'Brien grinned happily. He had a feeling Bashir's lucky streak—three winning nights in a row—was about to come to an end.

Dax sensed a hesitation in Myriam Kravitz as they stood in the doorway of Quark's place. A pair of inebriated Denuvians staggered past them, reeking of synthale, and Kravitz took a quick step out of their way. Her face showed distaste.

"You said you wanted to learn darts," Bashir was saying to Twofeathers. "O'Brien there is a true master of the sport. Taught me everything I know, in fact."

"I would like to meet him, then," Twofeathers said.

"Follow me." Bashir started forward, then paused. "Coming, Dax?"

Dax glanced at Ambassador Kravitz, then shook her head. "Not tonight. I'd like to find a quieter place. How about you, Ambassador?"

"I'll join you," she said.

"Great," Dax said. She gave Bashir a bright smile. "Next time."

Turning, she followed the Denuvians out. They headed up the Promenade toward their crossover bridge . . . probably planning to spend the night on their ship, she decided.

"Is it always so crowded there?" the ambassador asked, following her.

"Quark's? No, not usually. It's busy because of the negotiations."

She looked puzzled. "Aren't they private?"

"Of course. But there are quite a few Bajorans here to protest the Cardassian ambassador's presence. So the crews of the ships that brought them are here, waiting to bring them back. And there are interested observers from the Federation and, unless I miss my guess, from quite a few of the Maquis Homeworlds. Plus there's the normal station traffic. DS9 can get pretty full when something big is happening."

"Ah," she said.

"What kind of food do you want? There's a Klingon restaurant, but it's not for timid palates."

"I don't think so," she said. "I've heard about Klingon meals. I don't think I could eat something that's still moving. I'm more of a nice matzo ball soup type."

"In that case," Dax said, steering her toward the far side of the Promenade, "may I recommend the public replicators?"

Twofeathers deliberately missed the bulls-eye for the third straight time. He found it almost painful, in a way, to deliberately lose a contest. It went against his every instinct.

"Close," Bashir said. "You're catching on." He moved forward and removed the darts from the target.

"I need another drink," Twofeathers said.

"Charge whatever you want to the station's account," Bashir said. He returned to the throwing line, took aim, and let fly. The dart struck the tiny red circle at the center of the target: a perfect bulls-eye. The engineer—what was his name, O'Brien?—let out a loud groan.

"May I bring you something?"

"I'm still fine," Bashir said, throwing his second dart. It landed a hairsbreadth to the left of the first: another perfect shot. The doctor hadn't exaggerated, Twofeathers thought. He *was* an excellent dart player.

"I'm fine, too," O'Brien said, lifting his mug.

Twofeathers smiled and nodded pleasantly. Now was his chance, he thought, to make contact with Quark. He'd spotted the Ferengi behind the bar when he came in.

Weaving between the full tables, he reached the bar and pushed his way up to the front. Quark bustled over, looking harried.

"What can I get you?" he asked.

"Synthale . . . and a Mark III attack cruiser," Twofeathers said. "More, if you can get them."

Quark studied him. "Now where," he said, "would I get a Mark III attack cruiser?" he said.

"Bajoran military surplus. I know you have contacts."

Quark leaned forward. "How do I know you're not Federation security?" he asked in a voice barely audible over the background roar of the crowd. Twofeathers found himself straining to hear.

"The Grand Nagus's second cousin, Goff, sent me to you. He thought you might have a line on Bajoran war surplus. And by the way, he says you still owe him fourteen strips of gold-pressed latinum. Plus a ten percent commission for referring me to you."

"That sounds like Goff, always kidding." Quark laughed, but Twofeathers saw the greed in his eyes. "How long will you be here?" the Ferengi asked.

"As long as the peace negotiations take." Twofeathers leaned back. "I'm one of the Maquis ambassadors."

Quark nodded subtly. "Here's your synthale," he said, putting a mug on the counter and filling it from a pitcher. "I'll be in touch."

Twofeathers nodded, accepted his drink, and headed back for the dart game. Quark was hooked, he knew. Now it was all a matter of playing everything out to its all too inevitable conclusion . . . *victory.*

He began to smile.

Bashir aimed his last dart carefully, threw, and knew the second he released that it was another perfect shot. Sure enough, it hit the target dead center. "Yes!" he cried. "Game, set, and match!"

O'Brien groaned again. "That's quite a streak you have going," he complained as he went to retrieve the darts.

Bashir smiled. "Your game's off tonight," he said. "Is something bothering you?"

"I had a run-in with some Bajorans at the bar," he

said, and then he quickly explained what had happened. "They've been staring at me ever since."

"Don't worry, Chief, it'll blow over."

"I certainly hope so." He handed three darts to Bashir, then stepped up to the throwing line.

"You," a low voice growled. "You, the human." Bashir glanced back and found a Caxtonian approaching. It had a decidedly unfriendly look on its face, and he swallowed uneasily. He followed the alien's gaze . . . to Chief O'Brien.

"Uh, Chief . . ." he said softly.

"Not while I'm throwing, Julian," O'Brien said.

"I really think—" he began.

The Caxtonian knocked a chair out of the way and continued its inexorable advance. They weren't the brightest of beings, Bashir knew, but they made good pilots. They also never bathed, Bashir realized, as the smell of this one reached him: a sour-sweet reek of animal musk and sweat and decades of grime.

"—that you should look over here," he went on, still backing away. He tapped his badge. Better call for help now, he thought, before things got ugly. "Bashir to security," he said. "There's going to be a riot at Quark's. Hurry!"

O'Brien threw his dart. It not only missed the bulls-eye, it nearly missed the dartboard altogether, hitting a 5 point area in the outer ring.

"Look what you made me do!" O'Brien complained, turning. "So what is it, Julian, that's so damn important—"

"Human!" The Caxtonian seized O'Brien's tunic,

heaved, and in one motion sent him flying ten meters, across two tables, and into a knot of humans playing cards at a table. Poker chips flew in all directions. Players began to curse and pick themselves up.

Bashir saw shock on O'Brien's face and winced a bit in sympathy. That had to hurt, he thought. Luckily O'Brien didn't seem to have any broken bones.

"For my dead brothers!" the Caxtonian screamed. Then he headed for O'Brien again, shoving everyone and everything out of his way. Men and women began pushing and shoving one another in their haste to escape.

"Revenge!" the Caxtonian roared. "I kill you!" Clearly, Bashir thought, he had believed Quark's wild rumor.

Half a second later, the whole bar exploded with fists, flying chairs, and angry screams. Bashir saw O'Brien scrambling out of the Caxtonian's way, then a Bajoran leaped on the engineer's back. They vanished beneath a heap of bodies.

Bashir dove for cover. No sense getting hurt, he thought. He ducked as a half-empty bottle of Romulan ale came flying past and smashed to shards on the wall behind him. He had a feeling half the people here would need his medical services soon enough. How long till security arrived to break things up?

CHAPTER
11

AN ALARM SOUNDED aboard the *Progress*, and Odo returned to full consciousness with a jolt. What had happened? *Jem'Hadar?*

He poured himself up from the pail in a golden stream and allowed himself to coalesce into his usual humanoid form.

"What's wrong?" he demanded. He hurried forward to gaze out the front viewport. Stars blurred into lines around them from the distortion of their warp field. He didn't see anything out of the ordinary, but then he was a security officer, not a pilot.

"We've got trouble," Kira called from the pilot's seat.

"What sort of trouble?"

"Three ships," Worf said from the seat next to Kira's. He looked up. "Jem'Hadar, from their warp signatures. We are already within their sensor range. They are altering course to intercept."

"They're powering up their weapons systems!" Kira said. "Going to evasive maneuvers—"

"No!" Odo said. "Leave the ship on autopilot. Get into the back and hide. Get ready to activate your personal cloakers in case they board and search for you. I'll start the automatic distress call. We can fool them into leaving us alone."

Kira hesitated.

"Do it!" he told her. They didn't have time to argue. Why didn't humanoids ever do things the first time he asked?

Nodding, she ducked into the back section of the ship, and Worf followed. Chief O'Brien had done an excellent job of camouflaging the hidden compartments, and Odo felt certain they'd pass any Jem'Hadar inspection.

He slid into the pilot's seat and activated a low-powered distress call. The Jem'Hadar would pick it up, he knew. He was counting on it.

That only left himself. He flowed up onto one wall and changed into the shape of a support beam. It felt good to try a new form. He blended in so completely that not even the Jem'Hadar would be able to detect him.

From that position, he watched and waited with growing impatience. The largest of the three Jem'Hadar ships appeared on one of the monitors, approaching quickly from behind. It looked like an odd accumulation of spikes and rounded compartments placed on a huge boxlike ship. It was a design he had never encountered before. For a second he wondered if it could be a different species than the Jem'Hadar, but then he shook his head. No, it had to be them. Who else would be policing this sector of space?

Suddenly the *Progress* trembled all over—a tractor beam had locked onto them, he guessed. Their ship's engines automatically powered down to keep from burning out, and the sudden silence that filled the ship screamed more loudly than words. Suddenly they dropped out of warp, the stars in the front viewport changing from streaks of light to slowly moving dots. Then the Jem'Hadar ship began to pull them in toward a wide rectangular opening in its side . . . a landing bay of some kind, he guessed.

They passed through a series of force fields which cast shimmering blue lights across the monitors, and then they were inside, slowly settled onto what looked like a broad expanse of durasteel deck. Extruding a tendril of himself to get a better look through the front viewport, he saw rows of shuttles and small fighter ships lined up. There had to be dozens of them in this one landing bay, he realized. They were aboard some kind of transport ship. But did that mean well or ill for their mission?

Ten seconds after they touched down, he heard the airlock pop open. Quickly he withdrew his tendril from the front viewport, once again assuming the shape of a support beam.

Below him, a dozen Jem'Hadar troops stormed aboard, their disruptors held ready. He watched with interest as they advanced quickly through the cabin, covering one another, looking for any signs of life. They didn't discover the hidden compartments, he saw with relief. O'Brien's shielding held up. As they milled about, one of them produced a small black box with readouts on the top . . . a scanner of some kind, Odo thought.

A Jem'Hadar officer boarded last. He looked at the pilot seats, grunted once, then circled the seats in the main part of the cabin and peered into the back area. He frowned in puzzlement.

"Where are they?" he demanded of the Jem'Hadar with the scanner.

"There are faint life signs," the Jem'Hadar with the scanner reported. Odo felt a flash of panic. The shielding wasn't completely hiding Worf and Kira, he realized.

"Where?" the officer demanded.

"I cannot get a lock on it, sir."

The officer struck him backhanded across the face. "Fool. Give me your scanner."

The warrior handed it to him silently.

"They are hidden somewhere aboard," the officer announced. "Rip the ship apart. Find them."

"Yes, sir." Two of the warriors sprinted through the hatch. Probably going for heavy equipment, Odo thought. He'd have to do something. Even with their personal cloakers, Kira and Worf wouldn't stand a chance against a high-powered laser cutting through the bulkheads in search of hiding places. They'd be sliced to pieces.

"Is there anything else here?" the officer demanded.

"Just these," another trooper said, bringing out the message cube Sisko had given Odo back on DS9. He set it on a chair next to Odo's pail.

"Find out what it is," the officer ordered, handing the scanner back to the warrior he'd taken it from. "Is it a bomb?"

"No . . ." the Jem'Hadar said. "It appears to be a recording device of some kind."

Odo mentally nodded. *Come on,* he thought, *activate it—this might be the distraction Kira and Worf need to get out.*

The officer stepped forward and looked the box over suspiciously. Then he touched the button on the top. Instantly a holographic projection of Captain Sisko in full dress uniform appeared. He was bigger than life, towering a full half meter over the Jem'Hadar.

"I am Captain Benjamin Sisko, a Starfleet officer," Sisko's recording said in a booming voice. "This message is for the leaders of the Dominion. On behalf of the United Federation of Planets, I wish to invite the Founders to join us in a peace conference. This message box contains full instructions for getting a reply safely back to us, as well as all necessary diplomatic protocols this conference will require. We hope to meet with you soon."

The hologram disappeared as quickly as it appeared. It had been short and to the point, Odo thought. Hopefully it would be enough to fool the Jem'Hadar.

"A Federation trick," the officer sneered. The two Jem'Hadar who'd left reappeared, lugging what looked like a heavy-duty welding laser between them. "Tear the ship apart," the officer said. "Kill anything that moves. Find the source of those life readings."

"What about the box?" the Jem'Hadar with the scanner said.

"I'll take care of it." Drawing his disruptor, the officer took careful aim.

Odo knew this was the time to act. He couldn't let the message box be destroyed—not yet, anyway.

Letting his body change and flow like liquid gold, he dropped from the ceiling, then flowed up before them into his normal humanoid form. Folding his arms, he glared with all the strength he could muster.

The Jem'Hadar dropped to their knees before him. This, he thought, was a sign of the power the changelings wielded in the Gamma Quadrant.

"Your name," Odo demanded of the officer, trying to sound imperious.

"Sub-Garn Thok, Founder." He still didn't look up.

"I came personally to deliver this peace summit invitation, Sub-Garn Thok," Odo told them in the angriest voice he could muster, "in case anyone felt like intercepting it. I see my precautions were justified. Your superiors will hear of this. Leave my ship—

you are forbidden to touch it in any way. I will have need of it soon enough, when I return to the Alpha Quadrant."

"Yes, Founder," Thok said, still not looking up.

Moving with a confidence he didn't feel, Odo picked up Sisko's message box and stalked purposefully down the ramp and out of the ship. If he was going to be a Founder, he knew he'd better act the part—blustering, angry, and oh so superior.

Thok ran to catch up. Odo did not look back, but he could hear the rest of the Jem'Hadar warriors scrambling out the hatch as fast as they could.

"Sir," Thok said, "we had no idea you were aboard."

"Of course you didn't," Odo said. "That was the idea. I can see that I will have to deliver the peace summit invitation myself." He paused twenty meters from the *Progress* and turned slowly, surveying the vast landing bay. It had to be three hundred meters wide and easily fifty meters across. Perhaps as many as fifty small ships had been parked here. Suddenly he felt small and lost.

"Which way?" he asked.

Thok hurried to take the lead. "Follow me, Founder," he said, heading to the left, toward what looked like a bank of turbolifts on the far side of a pair of shuttles. "I will take you to a waiting place. Then I will let the captain know you are on board."

Odo nodded. That would do, for starters. He glanced back at the *Progress*. All of the Jem'Hadar had vanished, exactly as he'd ordered, and the ship now sat unguarded with its hatch open. At the very least he'd bought Worf and Kira some extra time.

Kira felt herself beginning to breathe again. If not for Odo, she knew they would have been caught.

Slowly she eased open the door to her hidden compartment and crept out. Worf joined her. She pantomimed looking out the hatch, and he nodded in agreement. They had to get out of here as fast as possible; no telling if Odo's orders would be countermanded by someone higher up.

Lowering herself to the floor, she crawled forward on her belly to the edge of the open hatch. There she peered out, taking in the long line of small starships standing between them and the far wall. Fifteen meters away, half a dozen gaunt, hairless, almost skeletal aliens with triangular heads appeared to be doing maintenance work on a small vessel. Then a line of Jem'Hadar warriors marched into view around another ship, and she ducked back to avoid being seen.

"We're not being guarded," she said in a low voice, "but there are plenty of people outside."

"We will never get this ship into space again," Worf said. "We must find another way to Daborat V."

"And we have to rescue Odo," Kira added.

"The mission must come first."

"I'm not leaving him." That was one thing you learned in the resistance: You took all your people with you when you left. She had no intention of abandoning Odo.

"We may not have that option," Worf pointed out.

Kira paused a heartbeat. One thing at a time, she told herself. For now, Odo could look after himself. Considering how the Jem'Hadar treated changelings, he wouldn't be in any immediate danger. They could save him later.

"We must find better cover," Worf said. "The Jem'Hadar may come back to check for us despite Odo's orders."

"All right," Kira said. She stood. "I'll go first."

She reached down and activated the cloaker beneath her blue dress. The controls were so simple, she could have operated them in her sleep. Just a little *push* and—

A shimmer of colors enveloped her, then grew clear. She found herself inside what appeared to be a bubble about twenty centimeters from her skin. She could see out, but murkily, as though through a thick glass wall, and all sounds suddenly took on a muted quality.

She glanced back and could just make out a dim form that had to be Worf. At least she could see him: She'd half expected him to be invisible to her, too.

"Don't lose me," she said, starting down the ramp. Eight minutes . . . that wasn't a long time. They'd better find a hiding place before then, she thought, or they were going to be in a great deal of trouble.

Odo watched the turbolift's readouts. They were rising rapidly, and when the doors finally opened onto a long corridor lit by bright overhead panels, he had counted seventeen decks. This Jem'Hadar spaceship was more enormous than anything he had ever seen before, practically a space-going city. Five or six DS9s would have fit inside with room to spare.

Thok stepped out ahead of him and ushered him forward to the sixth door on the left.

"Please wait here, Founder," he said, touching the hand pad. "I will inform my superiors of your presence."

The door dilated open, and Odo stepped into a tiny, almost unfurnished room. It had a narrow bunk, a small table that folded out from the wall, and a hard metal bench that was welded to the floor. There were no decorations or personal touches of any kind. He found it distinctly unpleasant . . . a cell more than anything else.

"What is this room normally used for?" he asked.

Thok stared at him, looking puzzled. "This is my cabin, Founder. You can rest comfortably here."

Odo swallowed and looked around again. He had always lived a life that others on DS9 considered austere, but compared to this officer's Spartan existence, he lived in decadent luxury.

"It will do," he said gruffly. For all he knew, this might well be among the nicest cabins on the ship, he reflected. The Jem'Hadar were notably lacking in decorator touches.

The door irised shut and he found himself alone. He glanced around again, then placed the message box on the table. Closing his eyes, he allowed himself to flow freely from one shape to another, mimicking everything around him . . . first the bed . . . then the table . . . then the bench . . .

Perhaps fifteen minutes later, the door opened again. Odo pulled himself back up into his humanoid form and found himself facing a new Jem'Hadar officer . . . this one considerably older than the other one had been.

"I am Jezrak, Captain of the *Sespar's Revenge,*" he announced, studying Odo with a calculating expression. Jezrak carried himself like someone used to being obeyed, Odo thought.

"My name is Odo," he said.

"I know, Founder. I have orders to bring you to the docking bay." He stood back away from the door. "This way, Founder. The others are waiting for you."

Others? What did that mean? *Other changelings,* a small voice inside him said. That had to be it. He swallowed. *It didn't take them long to get here.* But did that bode well for him?

Keeping his expression a careful neutral, Odo picked up the message box and stepped through the door. He would keep up his pretense of delivering the message, he decided, and see what happened.

Ten Jem'Hadar guards had been waiting outside. They fell in around him. Probably an honor guard more than anything else, he decided. They couldn't hurt him; their genetic programming made that impossible. And his own skills as a changeling—small compared to other members of his race, but huge next to solids like them—would be more than enough to save him in any emergency. No, he thought, the real danger would come from his own kind. He was the first changeling ever in history to have harmed another member of his own race. What if his people decided he had to be destroyed before he contaminated others of their kind?

He forced those dark thoughts to the back of his mind. He had no reason to expect trouble, he told himself. He'd have to see what developed. His main goal now had to be buying more time for Kira and Worf so they could carry out their mission. He could make it back to DS9 on his own later if he had to.

Jezrak escorted him back to turbolift, and they all rode back down to the huge open landing bay. As soon as he stepped out, he deliberately avoided glancing around for Kira or Worf; if they had any sense, they would have used their personal cloakers to get away from their ship and under cover by now, waiting their own chance to escape. He'd return to help them if he could, but that possibility seemed more and more remote.

"The others are waiting on their ship for you, Founder," Jezrak said. He started to the left, between a row of sleek little fighters, and after a half second's hesitation Odo followed.

They seemed to be heading for the largest ship there, a long, sleek white and silver craft. Its side hatch stood open, and a ramp had telescoped to the deck. Standing in the opening, waiting for him, were two changelings dressed in long, pale yellow robes. He didn't recognize either one.

Jezrak stopped at the foot of the ramp and folded his arms. Odo didn't see any other options, so he marched up to the open hatch with a confidence he didn't feel—best to play up his role, he thought. He would *be* the Federation's messenger. If he didn't act the part, they might suspect he had come here for other reasons.

The two changelings moved back, and he stepped between them and into the ship. It was nothing like he had expected. The main cabin was all white, from the floor to the walls to the ceiling, and two long, curved benches ran lengthwise down the cabin. It had no other furnishings. Between the benches, suspended in midair, hung a large holographic projection of a planet, which completely filled the center of the room. It was a beautiful world, Odo thought: deep azure oceans, four huge continents, tiny polar ice caps, all wisped with white clouds. Was that the new changeling Homeworld? He had no way of finding out, short of asking, and he wasn't quite prepared to do that yet.

He glanced forward, into the pilots' compartment. The four seats there were occupied by Jem'Hadar in black uniforms—pilots, Odo assumed. They didn't seem to be paying attention to anything behind them.

"You are Odo," one of the changelings said. It was a statement, Odo noticed, rather than a question.

"Yes," he said.

"I am Auron and this is Selann."

Odo gave them a quick nod. "I have come on behalf of the United Federation of Planets—"

"To deliver a peace message," Auron finished for

him. "We find it curious," he said, moving forward and taking the box out of Odo's hands, "that you did not come through more diplomatic channels, Odo."

"After the reception given to our last few ships," Odo said gruffly, "the Federation thought it prudent to come in more subtly this time."

"And to send you."

"That's right."

Auron set the message box on the floor, activated it, and watched impassively as Sisko's image appeared and repeated the peace initiative. When it ended, the changeling dismissed it with an idle wave of one hand.

"The Federation and the other powers in the Alpha Quadrant know our terms for peace," he said. "We will gladly take them under our protection. No other alternative is possible."

"Surely there must be room for negotiation."

"None," Auron said.

The hatch suddenly swung closed with a *whump* of displaced air, and Odo felt a sudden vibration running through the soles of his feet—the pilots had begun to power up the engines. He had a sudden sinking feeling inside as he realized Kira and Worf were about to be stranded here without him.

"Where are we going?" he demanded.

"Carnalia VIII," Selenn said. A shiver of sudden apprehension went through Odo as the changeling added, "A delightful little world, as you will soon discover."

CHAPTER
12

"BREAK IT UP in here!" a loud voice boomed, and a phaser hummed twice as it struck. A Caxtonian and a Klingon, arms locked around each other, fell to the floor.

That seemed to catch everyone's attention, Bashir saw. He watched as eight security guards jogged through the front doors of Quark's bar with phasers drawn and took up positions around the periphery of the fight. Although their weapons had undoubtedly been set for stun, Bashir knew nobody would want to be hit by them. Spending several hours unconscious, then waking up in a holding cell, was nobody's idea of a good shore leave, and most of the fighters looked like seasoned spacers.

"Break it up!" the lead security officer's voice boomed again. He was a Bajoran named Vertan,

officially Odo's third in command, but second until Lieutenant Commander Rodington returned from leave.

The rioters had all paused. Bashir saw fists unclench, chairs about to be thrown suddenly get lowered to the floor, and fallen comrades helped to their feet. Odo would have been proud of Vertan's work, Bashir thought.

"You will disperse!" Vertan called again. *"Leave the bar in an orderly fashion! Return to your ships! Anyone still on the station in five minutes will spend the night in a cell!"*

A few last bottles and glasses crashed to the floor, shattering, as the crowd headed for the doors. All, Bajorans, humans, Klingons, and aliens alike, gave the guards guilty glances as they passed by.

"Who's going to pay for this damage?" Quark demanded, appearing from behind the bar. "Arrest them!"

A stampede started. Quark could not have said anything to get them moving more quickly, Bashir thought. Security followed to make sure new fighting didn't break out. In ten seconds, only he, Quark, O'Brien, the Dabo girls, and the unconscious Caxtonian and Klingon remained. Then Ambassador Twofeathers poked his head up from behind the bar, smiled, and stood up.

"Most entertaining," he said.

Quark shot him a dirty look. "That's because *you* don't have to clean up the mess." He wandered out from behind the bar and stood surveying the damage and shaking his head. "Rom!" he bellowed. "Get a broom!"

Grinning, Bashir climbed to his feet, dusted himself off, and headed for O'Brien. Quark's brother, as always, would get the short end of the deal. Fortunately Vertan had arrived less than a minute and a half after the riot had broken out, so nobody had been seriously injured that he could see. Now, how much damage had that Caxtonian done to O'Brien?

Perched on the edge of a round table, O'Brien was gingerly feeling his right arm and grimacing a bit. No blood or broken bones showing, Bashir noted, looking him over quickly, although he'd have an old-fashioned black eye in the morning. Bashir pulled out his medical scanner and passed it over O'Brien's right arm, face, and chest.

"Wrenched shoulder," he said, studying the read-outs. "A few bruises. Just soft tissue damage, nothing to be concerned about. You'll be right as rain in a day or two."

O'Brien groaned loudly.

"Do you need something for the pain?" Bashir asked, frowning a bit. It shouldn't hurt all that much, he thought—had he missed something?

"I'm groaning," O'Brien said, "because I'm going to have to forfeit the game to you, Julian! I can't throw with my arm like this!"

Bashir grinned in relief, then quickly covered it up. "You're right," he said with mock seriousness. "But look at the bright side. Now you'll have an excuse when you lose to me, Chief."

O'Brien groaned again.

Quark scurried over, a stylus in his hand. "Did you see who started it?" he demanded. "I'm taking names!"

"Yes," O'Brien said. He slowly worked his shoulder in a circle. "I was there."

"Well?" Quark demanded, hand poised to write. "Who're responsible?"

"You are."

"Me?" Quark's expression of shock was priceless, Bashir thought. "I think you hit your head a little too hard there, Chief."

"It was that stupid rumor you started about me killing two Caxtonians!" O'Brien snapped. "When a real Caxtonian heard it, he decided to avenge his fallen comrades!"

Bashir made a tsk-tsk sound. "Sounds like you stuck it to yourself there, Quark."

"Everyone knows rumors don't count," the Ferengi said. "So, it was the Caxtonian . . ." He glanced over at the alien's unconscious form where it still lay. Bashir knew Vertan and his men would be back to collect the two bodies once they'd seen the other rioters safely off the station. "I have his ship's credit account number," Quark said. "They'll be getting a pretty sharp bill, I can tell you." He glanced around. "Six tables," he muttered, writing quickly. "Seventeen—no, make that eighteen chairs . . ." He wandered off, still taking notes of the damage.

"Tell me," Ambassador Twofeathers said, joining them, "is it always this exciting here? I joined the

Maquis in part for the adventure, but I have never seen anything quite like this before."

"This doesn't happen very often, fortunately," Bashir said. He glanced at the chronometer over the bar, which thankfully hadn't been broken by flying debris. It was nearly 2300 hours. "Maybe I should show you to your suite now, Ambassador. It's getting late, and I don't think much more is going to be happening here tonight."

Twofeathers nodded. "Yes . . . I think I'm done for now." He shot a quick glance at Quark. "Though I may be back tomorrow."

It was going to be a good day, Captain Benjamin Sisko thought. He awakened from a long, deep sleep feeling refreshed, almost rejuvenated. Rising, he showered quickly, shaved around his beard, and put on a dress uniform. His son, Jake, was still asleep, so he sat down to have a light breakfast of toast, orange juice, and strong black coffee. On the computer monitor, he called up the daily reports and flipped through them quickly.

A small riot at Quark's, but no injuries . . . sixteen ships queued up for docking today . . . no emergencies, no problems, no disasters. For once, the station seemed to be running smoothly on its own.

He wiped his mouth, stood, and put the dishes into the recycling bin. With everything going so well, he wondered briefly if he should tempt fate and stop by Ops on the way to the peace conference. After a second he decided he had the time. Besides, with everything going so well, what could possibly go wrong?

He tabbed his dress blouse closed at the throat and headed out. The second his door opened, he knew it was a mistake. A crowd at the end of the corridor spotted him.

"There he is!" someone shouted. Instantly a dozen people holding signs and placards rushed toward him. *Bajoran protesters,* he realized in dismay. They'd been staking out the habitat ring waiting for him, and now they'd found him.

Holding up both hands, he motioned for silence. "What is the meaning of this?" he demanded. "Protests are restricted to the Promenade. Clear this corridor at once or I will have you removed by security!"

A Bajoran man in a brown robe waved his people to silence. "A thousand apologies for the disturbance, Emissary," he said. "I am Vedek Werron."

"This is not the best time, Vedek." Sisko folded his arms, leveling a stern glare at the Vedek. He would have to handle this delicately, he thought. Werron might be an extremist and a reactionary, but he had quite a few followers.

"It's always the right time for justice!" Werron said loudly.

"Justice for Bajor!" the crowd began to chant. *"Justice for Bajor! Justice for Bajor!"*

"Vedek, there are channels for this sort of thing," he said, turning toward the turbolift at the far end of the corridor. He'd catch that one to avoid riding with any of the protesters. "Now if you'll excuse me, I have work to do."

"Of course," Werron said, catching up to him. "I'll just walk with you. I had something important I needed to tell you."

"What is that?" Sisko stopped and faced the Vedek with a sigh. He didn't seem to be taking the hint.

Vedek Werron drew himself up to his tallest, which still only came level to Sisko's shoulder. "I must demand that the Cardassians be put off *Deep Space Nine* at once," he said.

"That's impossible," Sisko said flatly. "We have delicate negotiations going on right now—"

"Gul Mekkar is the Butcher of Belmast." He whirled and addressed his followers. "And what do we do to Cardassian war criminals?" he shouted.

"Death!" the crowd roared.

"What else?" Werron cried.

"Justice! Justice for Bajor!"

Sisko tapped his badge. "Security," he said.

"Verton here, Captain," a voice said instantly.

"Get some people to the habitat ring," Sisko said. "Vedek Werron and his followers are staging a protest outside my cabin."

"I'll have people there in thirty seconds," Verton said. That was as good as Odo could have done, Sisko thought.

The crowd began chanting, *"Justice for Bajor! Justice for Bajor!"* again.

Smiling triumphantly, like he'd proved some point,

Vedek Werron turned back to Sisko. "Justice cannot be denied, Emissary," he said darkly.

"Of course," Sisko said. Over Werron's shoulder, he saw the turbolift doors open. Four human security officers sprinted up the corridor toward him. Verton had had the good sense to send humans rather than Bajorans, Sisko noted. Odo had picked the right man to leave in charge.

The security officers lined up two on each side of Sisko. Their hands were on their phasers, but they didn't draw their weapons yet. The were waiting for his go-ahead, Sisko realized. Hopefully it wouldn't come to that.

Werron's followers had begun to shift nervously, though. Good: He didn't want them getting too cocky with their protest. He didn't like being cornered.

"I'm not unsympathetic to the problem of Cardassian war criminals," Sisko said to Werron. "Many great injustices were done to your people during the occupation. Let me work through proper channels to look into the matter."

"When?" Werron demanded.

"How does this afternoon sound?"

Werron considered for a second, then nodded. "Thank you, Emissary," he said. "All we want is justice." Turning to his people, he held up his hands for silence. Instantly the chanting ceased.

"Join me for prayers and meditation," he said, cutting through them and heading for the turbolift. "The Emissary will help us!"

A cheer went up, and they followed him down the corridor.

Sisko relaxed. "See that they make it to the Promenade," he said to the security guards. "Then post a guard to make sure they don't hold any more impromptu protests on the habitat ring."

They nodded and followed Werron and his group. As soon as he was alone, Sisko turned and headed in the opposite direction. He'd take the other turbolift, he decided, to avoid any chance of running into any more of Werron's followers.

That still left his promise to fulfill. Tapping his badge, he said, "Sisko to Dax."

"Dax here," she replied.

Quickly he briefed her. "Find out all you can about Werron and his movement," he said. He would have done it himself, but he was going to be wrapped up with the peace negotiations all day.

"Easy enough," Dax said. "I'll tap into the Bajoran databases and see what they have on him."

"And see what you can find out about Gul Mekkar," Sisko added, "the so-called Butcher of Belmast. If Werron has a real grievance, I want to know it."

CHAPTER
13

KLINGONS WERE NOT meant for sneaking around, Worf thought in frustration. Their hands, their bodies—their very minds—were designed for clean, honest, open combat.

So what was he doing hiding in a small cleaning closet just off the landing bay? He rose and paced the few steps there was room for. There was no honor in hiding. If only their mission hadn't been so critical . . .

He glanced down at Kira, who was now asleep. She sat on the floor with her knees pulled up and her head resting on her arms, snoring softly. He snorted. How she could rest while being penned in here like some animal—

He shook his head. *Discipline,* he told himself, *is the heart of the warrior.* Kira was depending on him, and the future of the whole Federation might well depend on the success of their mission. He could wait in a supply closet for a few more hours.

At least the supply closet door had a few holes for ventilation. The air inside, thick with the scents of cleaning solvents, made him want to sneeze.

Rubbing his nose, he eased forward and pressed his eyes close to the top vent just in time to see a line of Jem'Hadar warriors jog up in formation to the calls of their superiors. He tensed as they turned and faced the supply closet, but then they moved into a drill of some kind.

Warm-up exercises, Worf thought. What better place to exercise than the open space of the landing bay?

He allowed his breathing to quicken. Martial arts had always been of keen interest to him, and he had tried everything from Klingon to human to Romulan to Doldarian forms of combat.

Their warm-up done, the lines of Jem'Hadar warriors suddenly broke into groups of four. Instructors passed among them, passing out wooden sticks about a meter and a half long. The foursomes began sparring.

Worf focused on one warrior, a tall Jem'Hadar who seemed to be single-handedly keeping the other three in his group at bay. He moved with the lightning reflexes of a natural athlete. Worf found himself tensing his own muscles as he sought to emulate what he was watching. Parry—parry—thrust—*kill!*

His breath quickened as he compared their moves to the Klingon martial arts he practiced. His respect for the Jem'Hadar as warriors began to increase. What other similarities to Klingons did they have, beyond their obvious love of battle?

He wanted to see more, but just as suddenly as the fights had begun, they ended. The Jem'Hadar raced back into formation, then began jogging farther down the landing bay. He listened, straining to hear, and heard the fighting beginning again, but he couldn't see it from the closet.

Frustrated, he turned and sank down to the floor. Idly he raised his tunic and glanced down at the cloaker. The readout said 00:05:14. Not much time left. He couldn't risk going outside to see . . . and anyway, someone might notice the door opening and shutting by itself.

"What was that noise?" Kira asked.

He glanced over and found her awake. "Jem'Hadar warriors training in the landing bay."

"Great," she said sarcastically. Opening her pack, she dug out a protein bar. "Want one?"

"Perhaps later," he said.

She opened it and bit. "I've been thinking," she said as she chewed. "If this ship follows the Jem'Hadar flight patterns that the Federation has been charting, it should enter the Daborat system in a day or two. That will be our chance to get out and find Orvor."

"This ship is too big to land," he said.

"Shore leave, Worf. Jem'Hadar have to go somewhere to burn off their energy. I'm willing to bet everyone goes down to the planet, leaving a skeleton crew watching things. We can sneak aboard a transport ship and ride down with them."

"You are forgetting how little time we have left on our cloakers," he said. He didn't think they'd have time to sneak aboard a Jem'Hadar ship and hide. And what if they were caught?

"Do you have a better plan?"

He hesitated. "Not yet," he said.

"Well, you have two days to think of one."

Worf leaned back and closed his eyes. Might as well rest, he thought. If he slept, the time would pass more quickly. And perhaps something would come to him.

A low rustling noise from his left brought him sharply back to consciousness. What was that? Kira, directly across from him, didn't seem to have heard it. Probably some small scavenger, he thought.

He turned and tensed. It wasn't some animal. A panel in the back of the closet was slowly sliding open.

Silently, Worf rose to his feet, gesturing frantically to Kira. She paused in midbite.

Then a small, gnarled-looking alien in a silver tunic slipped through the opening. Worf reached for his phaser. Whatever it was, it seemed to be sneaking up on them.

It took one look at Kira and Worf, let out an alarmed squeal, and bolted back into the opening.

Worf leaped forward and caught the door before it could slide back into place. He couldn't let the alien escape, he thought. He forced his shoulder through the opening, pushed, and managed to squeeze through.

He was in some kind of access corridor between the walls, he realized, taking in the unfinished walls and the bare metal floor. A few open panels revealed delicate-looking circuits and other equipment—kind of like the Jefferies tubes aboard a starship, Worf thought, only built to a practical scale.

The alien had dropped to four legs, sprinting like a wild hzork. Worf climbed to his feet, tucked down his chin, and raced in pursuit. Klingons were not known for speed or long endurance in wind sprints, but now Worf thanked his grueling workouts on the holodeck on the *Enterprise* and more recently in Quark's holo-suites. He was in top form. He actually started to gain ground on the alien.

The alien skidded around a corner and disappeared from sight. Worf put on a burst of extra speed, rounded the corner himself, and found the little alien prying open another access door.

"Got you!" he snarled, tackling it around the waist, trying to pin its arms. It bucked and twisted like a wild animal beneath him, hissing. It was stronger than it looked, Worf found, and he had trouble holding it down. Then it suddenly twisted its long, limber neck and sank its fangs deep into the flesh of his shoulder.

His whole right arm went numb. What—he thought, as a fuzzy-headedness spread through his mind. The alien wriggled out from under him. He tried to catch himself, but both his arms were completely numb. They hung like lead weights.

Distantly, he heard the hum of a phaser. With the last of his strength, he raised his head. Kira had stunned the alien, he saw. It fell just beyond him.

Good, he thought with satisfaction. He'd slowed it down enough for Kira to catch up with them. That was important. Now it couldn't betray them to the Jem'Hadar.

His vision grew cloudy, and he realized he was having trouble breathing. The numbness had reached his chest. He tried to suck in a deep lungful of air, but nothing happened.

"Kira—" he tried to say, but nothing came out. He could only gaze up at her with growing panic.

Then he felt his arms and legs moving on their own, shaking crazily, and his whole body began to convulse.

It was a short trip to Carnalia VIII, Odo found, and Auron and Selann made pleasant if innocuous (perhaps *too* innocuous, Odo thought darkly) conversation along the way. He found himself growing a little bored with their chatter about the weather on planets he'd never visited and about people he'd never met.

At last, though, the planet came into sight through the front viewport. Odo moved forward to see better. It was the same planet on the hologram in the center of the cabin, he realized, and he felt a growing sense of excitement. Was this the new changeling home? If so, the Federation would need to know its location.

Almost as if reading his thoughts, Selann came up

behind him and said, "We have a small outpost here, with few of the comforts of home."

"And where *is* home?" Odo said.

"With us." Selann smiled faintly. "You don't belong with the Federation, Odo. You know that deep inside."

"Perhaps," he murmured. He wasn't willing to give them any more encouragement than that, he decided. If he appeared too eager, they might catch on that he was hiding something. He'd only been off the Jem'Hadar ship for a few hours; Kira and Worf wouldn't have had time to do much of anything yet.

The pilots brought the ship down to a soft landing. Auron crossed to the hatch, opened it, and a sudden flood of deep amber sunlight entered the cabin. Odo followed Selann down the ramp.

They had landed in a cleared field, he saw. Thirty or so small white domes clustered to the far left, amid twisted treelike plants whose crowns held streamers of red flowers. A series of broad pebble paths threaded their way among the domes. He could see a number of changelings walking about over there, and he suspected that several of the trees might be changelings as well. He couldn't say what sixth sense told him; he just *knew*.

"Carnalia VIII," Auron said softly from behind him. "Stay with us here, Odo. Learn to use the power and influence that is your birthright."

"It's . . . tempting," he admitted. And it was. When he thought about all his people had accomplished, when he thought about the proud place they had made for themselves, he couldn't help but wonder what it would be like to join them.

Then he forced himself to back away from those thoughts. The changelings had accomplished a lot, but at too high a price, he thought. They had virtually enslaved an entire quadrant of the galaxy. That went against everything he knew to be right and good. He could never be a part of it. *Never.*

Selann smiled as they continued down the path to the domes. "This will be yours," he said, pointing to the third one.

The building had no door, Odo saw, just a large round opening in one side. He ducked through and caught his breath in amazement as he stared at the strange assortment of objects before him. Oddly shaped sculptures . . . intricate pottery . . . weathered stones . . . pieces of driftwood. No humanoid would like this dome, he thought, turning slowly to gaze in wonder at everything around him, but for a changeling it had a luxurious feel. On some level each of these objects called to him, asking him to emulate them.

"All this for me," he murmured.

"Yes," Selann said. "All this for you, Odo. You are one of us. You belong here. Join with me, Odo. Feel what it is to truly *belong.*"

He opened his arms to Odo, and Odo came to him. There was no way back to the Federation from here, no way to help Worf and Kira for the moment, so why not? He had joined with changelings before, when he'd visited their Homeworld, and it had been one of the most incredible sensations of his life. The nearest thing he could compare it to was sex among the solids, but it wasn't like that. It was . . . *spiritual,* he decided. A joining of minds, a melding of thoughts and souls, a surrender to a larger universe. You lost your individuality and became part of something greater than yourself.

As he watched his hands shifting, becoming golden, luminous, and liquid—as he felt his body merging with Selann's—his last thoughts were that he had indeed come home.

CHAPTER
14

KIRA FLIPPED WORF over onto his back and put her hands on his chest, trying to push him down. His whole body strained violently, almost knocking her off, and his arms and legs thrashed against the floor. Foam began to pour from his mouth and nostrils, and a weird pathetic wheeze came from his chest.

"Easy," she murmured, still pressing him down. "Easy, Worf."

His teeth clenched. He gave a low moan and relaxed, and for a second she thought the worst might be over. Then he began to buck again, moaning, his eyes rolling back in his head.

Finally his convulsions slowed, then stopped completely. Gasping for air, he lay still. Every few seconds, his legs or arms gave faint spasmodic twitches.

Was he dying? Kira bit her lip, then leaned forward

and put her head to his chest. His massive heart pounded wildly, but the beat seemed erratic to her. She sat back on her heels, trying to think. Battlefield medicine didn't cover situations like this one. If only Bashir were here. Should she try to get him to drink something? Or would that only make things worse?

Suddenly he gasped and opened his eyes. The pupils were bigger than she'd ever seen them before, and they were shot through with red lines.

"Worf?" she said. He didn't seem able to focus on her, though. "Can you hear me? It's Kira. How do you feel?"

"The corridor . . ." he whispered.

"What about it?"

"It is spinning . . ."

He raised one hand to his head. For a second he tried to sit up, but then he slumped to the side. He couldn't even lift his own weight, Kira realized with dismay. How was she going to get him down to Daborat V in this condition?

Carefully she eased her pack under his head for a pillow and dabbed at the foam around his mouth. The best thing she could do for him, she decided, was wait and hope for the best.

"Rest," she said softly. "I'm going to reconnoiter and see what I can find. Just as soon as I take care of our little friend here, that is."

Quickly she pulled a length of cord from her pack and tied up the little alien. He was still unconscious from the phaser stun, snoring loudly. Up close, he didn't seem very dangerous looking, but those tiny needlelike fangs and their venom had certainly done their work on Worf.

Was it part of the ship's crew? Searching its pockets, she found a brass ring, a few datachips, and some scraps of paper; all were dusty, battered, and looked like they had been lost for quite a while before being scavenged. No, she decided, the little alien couldn't possibly be a crewman . . . more like a mascot or a pet. If the Jem'Hadar kept pets, which seemed doubtful. Was it sentient? It had on a simple tunic, but that didn't mean much. They wouldn't know until it regained consciousness. Hopefully, whatever it was, it wouldn't be missed right away.

"Water," Worf said hoarsely.

She dug out a canteen and gave him a sip. Maybe that would help.

"How are you feeling?" she asked.

"Weak," he said. His voice was barely a whisper. "Help me sit up."

She carefully pulled him forward, then had him lean back against the wall. He had bloodstains on his tunic, she saw. Peeling it back at the shoulder, she found the two puncture marks which were still seeping red. Hard to believe, but those two tiny wounds had almost killed him.

"It seems he had some nasty venom in his fangs," Kira said. She pulled bandages from her pack and dressed the wounds.

"Fortunately," Worf said, voice stronger now, sounding more like his old self, "the effects do not appear long lasting on Klingons."

"Then I'll leave you to watch him and rest," Kira said. "I want to look down some of the tunnels. If we're going to be trapped here for a while, we're going to need to know the layout of the ship."

Worf nodded, wincing a little.

"I'll be back soon," she promised.

Rising, she turned and walked quickly back to the large tunnel that led to the storage closet. It amazed her how long and high they were. The access corridors seemed to run through the whole ship.

She explored, mentally mapping the place in her mind. Several times she came to ventilation ducts, and each time she peeked through. Once she saw several Jem'Hadar lying on rows of hard-looking bunks. Other times she saw empty rooms, or storerooms filled with crates.

She kept going and eventually came to the ship's galley. Through the ventilation holes, she could see long metal tables and benches. They seemed to be in the middle of a meal shift now; the benches were crowded with every species but Jem'Hadar, all eating what looked like nearly raw meat and some kind of vegetable stew. The Jem'Hadar didn't eat, she reminded herself, so there would be plenty of real food available. Perhaps they'd be able to sneak in during an off-shift; fresh supplies would make a good supplement to their protein bars, which they should hold for emergencies.

She checked the time. She'd been gone nearly an hour—time to get back to Worf. She didn't want to leave him too long in his weakened state in case any more of those savage little aliens showed up. He'd lived through one bite, but she didn't want to risk any more.

Retracing her steps, she neared to the corridor where she'd left Worf. Then from ahead she heard low voices. That could only mean trouble, she thought, drawing her phaser. If the Jem'Hadar had found Worf . . . she didn't want to think what it would mean. They weren't exactly known for their mercy or their compassion.

She crept forward cautiously, placing each foot carefully. As silent as Death, she peeked around the corner.

It was Worf talking to the little alien, she saw. Worf had untied their captive, and now the two of them sat facing each other. She relaxed and felt the tension drain from her shoulders. It seemed the alien was sentient after all.

"Major," Worf said, "I want you to meet Snoct Sneyd. He'd an Iffalian. Snoct, this is Major Kira."

"Hello," she said cautiously.

"Hello, Major Kira," Snoct said back, head cocked to one side in what might have been an almost comical manner in different circumstances.

"It seems I scared him when he stumbled upon us," Worf said. "He was part of a cleaning crew the last time this ship was serviced—"

"Six long months ago!" Snoct said.

"—and he fell asleep in our closet after a long shift. When he woke up, they were already in space."

"The Jem'Hadar have been trying to catch me ever since," Snoct said, "only I escaped."

"What do you mean, trying to catch you?" Kira asked. That didn't make much sense to her. "How could you elude the Jem'Hadar aboard their own ship?"

"I think it is a game to them," Snoct said. "They hold hunts for me, using primitive weapons like nets and spears."

"Have they never caught you?" Worf demanded.

"Once," Snoct admitted.

"What happened?"

"They let me escape."

"They *let* you escape?" Worf's knobby forehead furrowed.

"That makes sense," Kira said. "If it's a game to them, why let the fun end?"

"Because when the prey is caught, the game is over," Worf said.

"Haven't you ever wanted a game to keep going once it ended?"

"No," Worf said. "That would defeat the purpose of a game, which is victory."

Kira shook her head. Sometimes Worf just didn't understand. To Snoct, she said, "Do you know when this ship is due to visit Daborat V again?"

"I don't know," Snoct said.

"Can you take a guess?"

He mewed plaintively. "It could happen any time now. Today, next week, or six months from now. They don't confide in me, after all. I just hope it's soon. If they dock at any space station for servicing, I'll finally be able to escape!"

Without warning, a strange sound echoed through the corridors—a low, almost inaudible drumbeat, thumping just this side of subsonic. Kira felt the hair on the back of her neck start to bristle. Then came a drawn-out wail like the cry of someone being disemboweled.

Snoct let out a low moan.

"What's that noise?" Worf demanded, leaping to his feet. He balanced himself against the wall with one hand. He hadn't completely recovered from the effects of Snoct's bite, Kira realized.

"The Jem'Hadar have begun their hunt again," the little alien said with a shudder. "We must flee!"

CHAPTER
15

SHAKEN, ODO PULLED himself away from Selann and reassumed his own humanoid form. He had never known such peace, such tranquillity, as the first time he had joined with another changeling. It had left him weak from euphoria, almost giddy.

But this time it had been different. This time it hadn't been so novel, and he had been able to sense Selann's thoughts as they drifted between their collective consciousness . . . thoughts that bewildered and at times enraged him.

Thoughts of peace through conquest.

Thoughts of bending lesser races to his will.

Thoughts of a great destiny for their people and a vision of the future which Odo did not believe in—or want to share: nothing less than the conquest of the entire galaxy.

He took a step back, then another, then a third. All he wanted to do was separate himself from Selann, to put as much distance between them as he could.

Selann regarded him solemnly from the other side of the room. "Odo—" he said.

"Leave me!" Odo cried. "I cannot face your thoughts!"

Silently, Selann left the dome. Odo gazed at the statues and the driftwood, at the rocks and the pottery assembled around him. He no longer felt like emulating any of it. He just wanted to go home.

He heard a light step behind him and whirled. Had Selann returned? No, he saw, Auron had appeared in the doorway.

"Come with me, Odo," the changeling said softly.

Odo didn't know why, but he obeyed. He walked out with Auron onto the curving pebble path, and they passed in silence between the domes, through the trees, then onto a beach covered in glistening black sand. Low waves lapped at their feet, and the air held a faint tang of salt and brine. Far across the water, two huge orange suns sank toward the horizon.

"You are still not happy among us," Auron said, as they gazed into the distance side by side.

"I'm sorry," Odo said. "I cannot accept what you're doing. It isn't right—"

"Do not apologize," Auron said. "You are still

young, Odo. You have not seen all the horrors of the universe. You do not understand why we must stand united against the solids. But you will, Odo, in time. We are a very ancient and very patient race. We will wait for you to change, to see things as we do."

"It's just that my heart tells me all of this is wrong," Odo said. "Why can't all sentient life-forms find nonaggressive ways to live in peace everywhere in the galaxy?"

Auron laughed. "That's what we've done. All changelings live in peace. No changeling but you has ever harmed another. It's only the solids who are a threat and must be restrained."

Odo sighed and shook his head. His people didn't want to understand, he realized. Perhaps they had grown too comfortable with their power, or too drunk on their success. He had to escape. He had to find some way to return and help Worf and Kira if he could. But how?

"Perhaps," he said hesitantly, "if you could show me more of what you've done here, in the Gamma Quadrant . . .?" Maybe he could persuade Auron to take him to Daborat V, he thought.

"Of course," he said. "We will take you on a tour of the nearby worlds so you can see how well everything is run. Perhaps then you will come to understand the magnitude of what we have accomplished here, and what we will accomplish in the future, when you rejoin us. The Alpha Quadrant is ripe with possibilities, Odo, and with your knowledge and secure position within DS9, you can be of invaluable aid."

"Perhaps," Odo said, but he swore to himself that he would never let that happen.

"This way," Auron said, heading back toward the domes. "We will leave at once."

CHAPTER
16

THE CONFERENCE HAD been scheduled to start promptly at 09:00 hours. Sisko arrived at the proper section of the habitat ring fifteen minutes early, determined to get everything off on the right foot. His run-in with Vedek Werron had soured his mood, but whatever coddling the ambassadors needed to get things rolling, he would provide it. Admiral Dulev had been more than clear on that subject, and he planned on taking no chances with these negotiations.

The four security guards posted in the corridor outside the conference room snapped to attention the second they saw him.

"Status report, Ensign?" he asked the closest, a tall, fair-haired man whose name he recalled was Dan Cziraky.

"None of the ambassadors has arrived yet," Cziraky said. "Security measures are all in place. The room hasn't been left unguarded for a second, sir. Only Quark has been inside, and I accompanied him."

Sisko frowned. "Quark?" he asked. Now, what would the Ferengi want in the negotiation room?

"He dropped off the refreshments, sir," Cziraky said. Sisko nodded. He vaguely remembered signing off on the requisition. "I accompanied him the whole time. And I screened everything he brought in with a tricorder. There were no poisons or listening devices, sir."

"Very well," he said. "Keep up the good work."

Punching his access code into the hand pad, he surveyed the room when the doors slide open. A square table three meters across had been set up in the exact center, with place cards indicating assigned seats. The Federation negotiating team would have their backs to the door, facing the Maquis members; to the left would be the Valtusians and to the right the Cardassians. Sisko would sit in as an observer on the Federation side of the table whenever he joined them. Four extra chairs sat against each of the side walls.

He circled the table, looking everything over one last time. A small table at the back of the room held various pitchers of drinks—water, fruit nectars, juices—and a selection of small pastries, thanks to Quark. There were plenty of padds for note taking . . . in short, everything the ambassadors could possibly want. He nodded to himself. Everything seemed perfect. Now, if everyone would only agree on peace. . . .

The doors opened suddenly, and he turned to find the Cardassian negotiators filing into the room, led by Gul Mekkar. Mekkar dressed in a slate gray shirt and pants, with a silver belt and more silver trim on his sleeves and shoulders. The other two Cardassian ambassadors—both women—dressed much the same way.

Mekkar took one look at the table and sneered, "This is totally unacceptable."

Sisko sighed inwardly. "What's wrong?" he asked in a deliberately even tone. Mekkar's reaction did not bode well for a timely start to the negotiations, he thought. "If any changes are needed, of course we will be happy to comply."

"We must be seated facing the door, at the head of the table," Mekkar demanded. "And furthermore—"

No, Sisko thought, as his head began to throb, it looked like it was going to be a long opening session.

Jadzia Dax had always had an affinity for research work. Perhaps it stemmed from Jadzia's days as a novice, before she got her symbiont. In her youth, she had spent most of her studies on computers, locked away from people, reading and researching. Now that she had been joined with her symbiont, the part of her that had been Curzon Dax—adventurer, explorer, and rogue—she realized how foolish that choice had been. You had to embrace the wonders of the universe, get out of your house and off your planet, explore the

galaxy and experience new things. The joining of
Jadzia and the Dax symbiont had produced little in
the way of new research, but she still had her old
skills, and now it was time to put them to good use.

Accessing Bajor's computer systems, she began a
global search for anything to do with Vedek Werron's
career. Almost at once a stream of articles began to fill
the computer's memory buffer. She punched up the
most recent and skimmed it quickly. It told of his trip
to DS9 to protest Gul Mekkar's presence. In fact, she
discovered as she read one article after another, all of
the recent stories seemed political in nature—the
Vedek's somewhat controversial interpretations of
prophecies, the protest marches he led in the capital,
that sort of thing. The Prophets could be interpreted
quite a few different ways, she knew, but the Vedek's
take on them seemed rather . . . *militant* might be a
good word, she finally decided. It seemed he'd taken a
personal interest in bringing Cardassian war criminals like Gul Mekkar to justice, and he used the
ancient Bajoran prophecies to justify the often extreme nature of his actions.

As she continued to work her way back through the
news stories, she found the articles suddenly stopped
about a year previously. It seemed almost as if Mekkar had appeared out of nowhere. That threw up
warning flags, so she jumped back to the earliest
article in the buffer and read more deeply into the
story.

It told how Vedek Werron had emerged from an
extended period of meditation. He claimed to have

had a new series of visions from the Prophets after spending nearly twenty years—most of his adult life—in secluded meditations in the Retollan Monastery on Bajor. His sudden emergence and very public life had caused something of a stir in Bajoran religious circles. Kai Winn had been particularly critical of Werron and his visions, but then, Dax reflected, Winn was critical of anyone whose views didn't match her own. For all Dax knew, Kira would have put that down as a mark in Werron's favor.

Vedek Werron appeared completely on the level as far as his presence on DS9 was concerned. Dax rose, crossed to a replicator, and got a glass of prune juice. She sipped as she sat back down, then grimaced a bit. Not her favorite among the human fruit juices by any means, she decided. Still, she'd overheard Worf claiming it was a drink fit for a warrior, and she'd always had an interest in the Klingon way of doing things. She sipped again, a little more deeply, and this time the flavor didn't seem so bad. In fact, she thought, it just might begin to grow on her, in time. . . .

She returned to her reading. Now, who exactly was this "Butcher of Belmast" he claimed to be stalking?

The negotiating session was not going well.

Sisko, sitting next to Ambassador T'Pao on the Federation side of the table, had developed a splitting headache. If he heard Mekkar whine one more time about protocols, he thought he'd scream. And the same went for the Federation ambassador, Harold

DuQuesne. The Maquis and the Valtusian ambassadors sat in near silence, watching with what Sisko could only assume was amazed shock as questions of who sat where, who spoke first, and whether the table was really big enough or the right shape or the right height were argued back and forth in mind-numbing detail and at sometimes deafening volumes.

It was amazing, Sisko thought, that peace had ever been declared between Cardassia and the Federation. Heaven save us from diplomats, as his father might have put it.

"These matters are irrelevant," one of the Valtusians finally announced, and the three ambassadors rose as one. "Summon us when you are ready to talk."

Sisko stood, too. "Ambassador," he began. Zhosh regarded him with an unblinking green eye. "I will call you as soon as possible," Sisko said.

The Maquis ambassadors followed the Valtusians out. Twofeathers had been shaking his head in disgust. "Fools," Sisko overheard him murmuring to Ambassador Kravitz, "I *told* you this would be a waste of time—" Then the doors closed, leaving the Federation and the Cardassian ambassadors alone.

"Can't we wrap this up?" Sisko demanded.

T'Pao leaned over and whispered in his ear, "The first side to surrender on a point of protocol loses a vital edge in negotiations, Captain. Have patience. We know what we are doing."

Still the debate raged back and forth. Finally Sisko recessed for lunch, and when they reconvened an hour later, nothing had changed.

At last the Cardassians gave in on the table: The present height and dimensions would be acceptable. The Federation gave in on the seating order, and everyone exchanged places, with the Cardassians now sitting at what they considered the head of the table, with the Federation to their left, the Valtusians to the right, and the Maquis facing them.

Mekkar seemed to be gloating inwardly about this supposed victory, Sisko thought. It made him bristle, and when he glanced at T'Pao, DuQuesne, and Strockman, none of them seemed entirely comfortable . . . though it was hard to tell with a Vulcan.

"Agenda next," the Valtusian ambassador said.

"That's another problem," Mekkar began.

Sisko sighed again. They really didn't need him for this, he thought. It was almost time for the session to end for the day, and he had important duties to attend to.

He leaned over to T'Pao and said softly, "Nothing is going to be accomplished today. Please call me if you need me."

"Affirmative, Captain," she said, equally softly. "However, you are mistaken. In the initial jockeying for position, we have achieved a minor victory."

"I'll take your word for that." Sisko rose. "Good day," he said, nodding to everyone else in the room. "Station duties call, but I trust I will hear from you if you have any comments or suggestions."

"You can count on that," Mekkar said.

I'm sure I can, Sisko thought.

He strode from the room, and the moment the door closed behind him, he let out a deep sigh and rubbed his temples. How could T'Pao possibly think they had accomplished anything? He crossed to the turbolift and a second later one came.

"Ops," he said to the computer.

It whisked him to his destination, and ten seconds later he stepped out into the familiar bustle of the nerve-center of *Deep Space Nine.* He surveyed the men and women moving about their tasks, monitoring their stations, and generally keeping the business end of the space station going. There were no arguments or egos at play here; it felt good to be back.

"Benjamin," Dax called, "I have that information you wanted."

"In my office," he said, and he led the way.

As he settled into his chair, he realized his headache had vanished. Five minutes away from Gul Mekkar was all it had taken. If only Bashir could bottle that, he thought a bit wryly.

"What have you got for me?" he asked.

She held up a datachip. "Every news report from Bajor that mentions Vedek Werron."

"Give me the short version." He leaned forward, interested.

"He is apparently something of a militant outsider in Bajoran political and religious circles—if there's a difference these days—due to a series of rather extraordinary visions he claims to have experienced during a twenty-year seclusion in a Bajoran monastery."

"A twenty-year seclusion? That sounds a little odd," he said.

"It gets better," she said. "He suddenly emerged from that seclusion one year ago, when he began a crusade to capture and punish all Cardassian war criminals. He has surrounded himself with a band of militant radicals, and several times Kai Winn has had to publicly chastise him for his zeal."

Sisko frowned, considering the facts. Changelings could disguise themselves as anyone, he knew, and the Bajorans weren't equipped—mentally or technologically—to defend themselves against that possibility. If a changeling wanted to infiltrate DS9, what better way than through a Bajoran religious figure? How hard would it be to replace a Vedek who hadn't been seen in public in twenty years?

If they had Vedek Werron set up as a "sleeper" of some kind, what better time to use him than now? If they could disrupt the peace talks, it might well prolong the Maquis conflict and keep the Alpha Quadrant divided and weak and therefore ripe for attempted invasion and takeover.

"Are you thinking what I'm thinking?" he asked.

"That he could be a changeling? The possibility did occur to me."

"Good, then I'm not paranoid." He tapped his badge. "Sisko to Bashir, please report to Ops." Suddenly he wanted a DNA scan run on Vedek Werron.

"Right away," came the doctor's response.

"You know how touchy the Bajorans are about their religious figures," Dax said.

Sisko nodded. Bashir couldn't just walk up to one and demand a cell sample. That would be a good way to start a riot.

"I'll just have to rely on the good doctor's wits and subtlety," he said. He knew Bashir liked to play spy in Quark's holosuites. He'd heard quite a tale of it from Garak while the Cardassian tailor was letting out his uniform a bit the other week. Now was the time for Bashir to use those finely honed skills in real life.

CHAPTER
17

"QUIET!" WORF HELD up one hand, straining to hear. A Klingon's senses were more acute than a human's, he knew, so he stood a better chance of detecting any dangers that might lie ahead of them.

The weird cry came again, echoing through the corridor like a brush-devil's hunting scream. It sent shivers of anticipation down Worf's back. He had only hunted brush-devils once, on the Homeworld with his brother Kurn, but it had been one of the most satisfying experiences of his life.

He glanced back. Kira and Snoct had paused, hardly moving, hardly breathing. Snoct looked frightened nearly out of his wits. They would have to get to safety soon, he thought. The corridors seemed to be rapidly filling up with Jem'Hadar warriors, all giving hunting cries.

Worf slowly leaned forward, turning his head ever so slightly. As he'd thought, below the loud cry he heard the mutter of voices from just ahead, along with an odd whisking sound that he couldn't identify.

He felt Kira tap his arm and, frowning, he glanced back at her. She pantomimed a broad shrug. Of course, he thought, with her poor hearing, she wanted him to tell her what was going on.

"Jem'Hadar ahead," he breathed, the barest of whispers. It sounded far too loud to him.

"Flee!" Snoct whimpered. The little alien turned to run, but Worf snagged his arm with a lightning move.

"You *will* be safe with us," he promised. "Stay." It was an order, not a suggestion.

Snoct's limbs were trembling violently, but he managed a nod of assent. Worf released him, feeling a twinge of disgust. Snoct was a coward, little better than a spooked herd animal. Although he realized the little alien couldn't help it—indeed, fleeing in terror seemed to be his normal reaction to any confrontation or surprise—such a response was so alien to the Klingon way of life that Worf just couldn't accept it. There had to be something Snoct could do to bolster his nerves. For now, though, it was enough that he wasn't running down the corridor shrieking in hysterical panic.

Carefully Worf peeked around the corner. Fifty meters away, a group of seven Jem'Hadar warriors was strolling toward him at a leisurely pace, laughing and joking among themselves. Worf inhaled sharply—their clothing was anything but standard: jungle-green kilts and leather sandals with thongs that laced up their legs. Their chests and faces had been painted with green geometric shapes. Strangest of all, for weapons, the Jem'Hadar held what looked like wooden spears. The whisking noise was them sharpening the tips of those spears with stones as they walked.

As he watched, they reached a small side corridor. There they all paused, and two of their number leaped down the passage, giving that strange warbling cry. A second cry answered from farther down that side corridor. Another hunting party? Worf assumed so.

A few moments later, the two rejoined their group. They pantomimed throwing their spears with exaggerated hops and bounds, to the hoots and cheers of their companions. A few Jem'Hadar now pulled small nets from their belts and began whirling them overhead until they made a whistling sound. The rest cheered like it was all some wild, drunken game.

Suddenly he realized that it *was* a game to them, like Kira had said. They were hunting Snoct Sneyd for sport. But that was only part of it. This was a bonding ritual, a way for warriors to grow closer to one another. Everything made sense to him now. It didn't matter if the hunt succeeded or not—it was the act itself that they found important.

They gave another series of hunting calls. The noises were designed to spook game animals, Worf decided, to send them fleeing in panic. Kurn had done that with the brush-devil, driving it toward Worf that day on the Homeworld. And it was working just as well on Snoct.

Satisfied he understood, Worf leaned back. "They're trying to drive us out into the open," he said to Kira. "They must have set a trap."

"We can't run into it blindly," Kira said.

"We must fight them," Worf said. He stretched, feeling his muscles ripple like liquid durasteel. Only seven Jem'Hadar and they looked inebriated. How would they stand up against one sober Klingon warrior? Not well, he thought.

"Not a chance!" Kira said. "That's a fast way to an early grave."

"They are only carrying spears and nets," he pointed out. "We have phasers."

"If they fail to return, dozens or perhaps hundreds of Jem'Hadar will come looking for them."

"I suppose *you* have a plan," Worf said. He readied his phaser. "They will be here in a few moments."

Snoct whimpered again and started edging away. Kira reached out, grabbed his arm, and hauled him back. Worf shook his head with distaste; Snoct had begun shaking in fear again. He had never seen such a cowardly creature.

"Damn right, I have a plan," she said. "Since the Jem'Hadar are in the access tunnels, who's going to be outside in the ship's main corridors?"

"The crew—" Worf began.

She shook her head. "With this many people hunting for us, a skeleton crew must be running the ship.

Every off-duty Jem'Hadar is probably in on the hunt."

Worf pondered that for a second. It sounded reasonable. Of course they would all want to take part in the sport and the bonding ritual. He would have felt the same way if Sisko held similar rituals aboard DS9—which might be a good idea to suggest once they got back.

"Where do you think we should go?" he asked.

"Back through the cleaning supply closet, assuming we can get to it safely, and then out into the landing bay."

"Our ship—"

"It's a possibility."

"I will go first," Worf said, heading back down the tunnel. Now that they had a plan, he could act on it.

Periodically he glanced back to check on Kira, and each time he found her following, still clutching Snoct's arm in a vicelike grip. Good; she wasn't taking any chances in letting him get away.

At each intersection Worf paused, listening. Any time he heard sounds of Jem'Hadar hunters, they skirted them. Once, in a darkened section, he saw bright lights approaching from the left. He led them back, crouched in the recess with Kira and Snoct until a hunting party of six Jem'Hadar passed, then led them forward once more.

Finally, after what seemed hours, they reached the access panel leading to the cleaning supply closet. Worf pressed his ear to the panel and listened intently. He heard not a whisper of a sound from the other side; it had to be empty. Leaning his shoulder to the panel, he pushed until it snapped out of position, then slid it smoothly to the side.

"Quickly," he said.

Kira released Snoct who promptly turned and bolted blindly up the corridor.

Worf dove after him and just managed to snag the back of the little alien's tunic. Snoct whirled, fangs snapping, and Worf slapped him open-handed across the face. Hissing, Snoct drew back to strike again, and this time Worf shook him like a rag doll. He wasn't taking any chances of getting another bite from the little alien; once had been more than enough.

At last Snoct went limp. A series of small sobs shook his body.

"It will be all right," Worf said, trying to sound reassuring. In some ways, Snoct reminded him of his son Alexander. He could still remember the times on the *Enterprise* when Alexander had awakened screaming from nightmares. Comforting his son had been a new and somewhat awkward experience. But he had learned the technique from necessity. "It will be all right," Worf said again. "I will not let them hurt you."

The warbling cries of the hunters grew louder.

"Let me go!" Snoct whimpered. "Let me go!"

"Not a chance," Kira said. Worf noted idly that her voice held far less sympathy than his. She ducked through the opening into the cleaning supply closet. "Pass him through," she said to Worf.

Worf, holding Snoct one-handedly by the back of his tunic, pushed him through the opening, then when

Kira had him safely restrained, Worf climbed through himself. Turning, he eased the access panel back into position. When it snapped into place, the cries of the Jem'Hadar hunters became nearly inaudible. They were safe, at least for the moment, he decided.

He glanced around. Nothing had changed in the supply closet, and he still found the stench of chemicals and cleaning solutions overpowering. He rubbed his nose and tried to ignore a sudden urge to sneeze. At least Snoct had stopped shaking, he saw, and now huddled quietly in the center of the room. The closet seemed to be something of a safe haven for him.

Kira crossed to the door into the landing bay and opened it a crack. A bright blade of light cut across the room. Worf straightened, listening intently, but nothing more than the low constant thrum of the ship's engines reached him.

"It's deserted," Kira said, peeking out, "exactly as I'd hoped."

She opened the door fully, and Worf gazed out into the flight bay. It stretched hugely before them. Not a single Jem'Hadar was in sight, but a new ship had docked, he noticed. It was a small, sleek-looking white craft with three warp nacelles over an ovoid cabin. He'd never seen anything quite like that design before. It certainly hadn't been made in the Alpha Quadrant.

He noticed Kira eyeing the new ship, too. "What do you think?" she asked softly.

"If we can get it out . . ." he mused. It might be exactly the sort of vessel they would need to get to

Daborat V, he realized. It looked fast. And if the changelings had installed one of the cloaking devices they'd stolen from the Romulan fleet they'd destroyed, it could well be the answer to their problems.

"Shall we take it?" he asked.

Kira hesitated. "Not yet," she said, "but I think it's going to be the safest place to hide."

"Agreed," Worf said. The last place the Jem'Hadar would think to search would be another ship. "What about Snoct?" he asked.

"Bring him," she said. "He wants off this ship as badly as we do."

"Thank you!" Snoct called, leaping to his feet. "Thank you!"

"We will not be able to use our personal cloakers if there are three of us," Worf pointed out. "It is a long way across to that ship."

"I don't think we'll need them. Cover me." Kira took a hesitant step out from the storage room, looked up and down the broad expanse of the landing bay, then turned and walked with calm precision toward the new ship.

She reached it unchallenged, entered the open hatch, and disappeared from sight. Worf strained to hear. He didn't like not being able to see her.

Snoct crowded up against him, and he let one hand drop to the little alien's shoulder. If Snoct tried to flee again, he'd be ready for it, he thought.

"Let me go!" Snoct said, sounding like his old self once more. He had completely stopped shaking.

"Will you run?" Worf asked.

"No."

Worf narrowed his eyes, studying the little alien. Snoct seemed in complete control of himself now. How would Deanna have handled it? She would have analyzed Snoct's motives, he thought. Undoubtedly she would have concluded that he suffered from a strong panic-flight impulse. Now that Snoct was no longer confronted by an immediate threat, his rational mind had resumed control. But how long would it last? Worf wished he knew. *Probably until we encounter another danger,* he thought.

"Let me go, please, friend Worf!" Snoct said again.

"Very well," Worf said a little reluctantly. He couldn't fight effectively while shepherding the little alien anyway, and Kira might need him any second now. "But I *will* be watching you," he added in his most menacing growl.

Kira finally reappeared in the little shuttle's open hatch and beckoned them forward. She hadn't drawn her weapon, he noticed, which seemed a good sign.

"Come," Worf said. Drawing a deep breath, he jogged away from the storage room door, heading for the shuttle. Suddenly he realized he didn't hear Snoct's footsteps behind him and, with a silent groan, he glanced back.

Calmly, the little alien was shutting the storage room's door behind them. Worf could have slapped himself; he should have thought to do that. When Snoct finished, he dropped to all fours and sprinted after Worf.

Worf made it up the ramp and into the ship. It had

only been a hundred meters, but he felt his heart racing. He would double his workouts when he got back to *Deep Space Nine,* he vowed, to get into better shape. A Klingon warrior's heart should be beating almost normally after a dash like that.

A second later Snoct joined him. The alien panted, long forked tongue flicking in and out between his fangs.

"Well?" Worf asked Kira.

"It's perfect," she said. "This ship has the range to make it to Daborat V and back to the Alpha Quadrant."

"Do you mean to steal it or to hijack it?" Worf asked, brow furrowing. Both possibilities had their advantages, he thought. Hijacking the ship after it had launched would mean fighting and prisoners. But trying to steal it from the flight bay might be even harder. He felt no qualms about taking the ship either way; the Federation was at war with the Dominion, and this would be a military action, he reasoned, rather than theft in the traditional sense.

"I'm not sure which would be easier," she admitted. "We'll have to see what opportunities present themselves. Our first goal remains getting safely to Daborat V. We still have to meet Orvor there. For now, I think we should stow away here and see what develops."

"By the time this ship is launched, we might be halfway across the Gamma Quadrant!"

"I think it's a chance we should take," Kira said. "We can't guarantee that *any* Jem'Hadar ship will land on Daborat V, but given the size and proximity of that base, I think it's a good possibility."

Worf considered that. True, Daborat V was an important world in the Dominion, and it held the largest Jem'Hadar base in this sector. Logically, it might well be the little ship's next destination.

"But if it is not the destination . . ." he began, looking at her sharply.

"If it's not," she said, "we'll take the ship on a little detour. By force, if we have to."

Worf nodded. It was a good plan, he decided.

Kira led the way toward the rear of the ship. It had been divided into three compartments, Worf saw. Four seats occupied the smaller front compartment, facing control panels and the broad curved viewports. The second compartment held two long slightly curved benches, separated by a wide aisle; the walls were white and made of some sound-dampening material, as were the floors and ceiling. The third compartment held storage lockers, the warp drive, and controls for all of the ship's other systems.

The lockers, he saw at once, offered the most cover. He opened the nearest one and peered inside, sniffing. A faint odor of mold greeted him, and something had left a greasy stain on the floor. Other than that, it was empty. At least it was tall enough that he could probably squeeze inside with a minimum of trouble, he thought.

He eased his right shoulder in, tucked down his head, and crammed himself in as best he could. Kira pushed until the door shut and the latch clicked. He could see out a little bit through the narrow ventilation grills cut into the metal.

"How is it?" she asked.

"Bearable," he said. He wouldn't want to spend much time locked in here, though.

Suddenly Snoct Sneyd dashed into the rear of the shuttle. "They're coming!" he shouted in near hysteria. "They're coming!"

"Who?" Worf demanded through the locker.

"Jem'Hadar!"

"Stay inside, Worf," Kira said to him. "I'll get Snoct out of sight and hide myself. This could be it!"

"Hurry," he told her. He dropped his hand to his phaser. If she couldn't get under cover in time, he would leap out to help defend her.

He watched through the vents as she forced Snoct into another empty locker, then climbed into one herself and shut the door.

She barely made it in time. Worf discovered he could see about half of the passenger section and a third of the cabin where the pilots sat, if he pushed himself all the way back against the far wall of the locker. He felt the metal start to bend beneath him and forced himself to relax. This was going to be a long trip, he told himself. He wasn't looking forward to it. Already his muscles had begun to ache from confinement.

One by one he began to tense his muscles, going through an ancient Klingon exercise designed to keep his body from stiffening up. It was the only thing he could think of that might keep him fighting fit while crammed in such a tight space.

From her locker, Kira had a clear view all the way to the front of the little ship. She watched with growing uneasiness as first one, then another, then a third Jem'Hadar entered. Two slipped at once into the pilot and copilot seats. The third turned to gaze outside at whoever was coming up the ramp next.

Great, she thought, *it looks like we're going to have a large traveling party.* Had she been insane, suggesting they try to hijack this ship?

But instead of more Jem'Hadar, a pair of changelings climbed aboard . . . and the second one, she was shocked to find, was Odo.

CHAPTER
18

AT 1530 HOURS, Captain Sisko walked into the negotiation room again. Ambassador T'Pao had called him in his office and asked him to join them once more. "All matters of protocol have been settled," she had reported.

"Excellent," he had said. "I take it the Valtusian and Maquis ambassadors have also been notified?"

"Of course."

"I'll be right there."

When he walked into the room, Ambassador Zhosh was speaking. Sisko felt a brief stab of disappointment that they hadn't waited for him, but just as quickly he realized how silly that was. He had no official standing here; they didn't have to wait for him. Sliding into his chair, he gave T'Pao a brief nod.

"—will create a self-governing buffer zone for the

disputed worlds," Ambassador Zhosh was saying. "Neither the Federation nor the Cardassians will have jurisdiction here. The Maquis will be transformed from a military agency to a political one, under the supervision of both the Federation and Cardassia, with duties that include policing their own worlds."

"A bold idea," Harold Strockman said from the Federation side of the table.

"Indeed," Gul Mekkar said, "but I fail to see why Cardassia should be the only one to give up anything in such negotiations. These are *our* worlds, in an area of space which is under *Cardassian* rule."

"They are *our* worlds!" Ambassador Twofeathers cried, leaping to his feet. "We never asked for Cardassian rule!"

"But," said Mekkar, a trifle smugly Sisko thought, "you *are* Cardassian citizens now."

"Please." Ambassador Zhosh looked at each side with one eye. "Resume your seats. We have not yet finished."

Reluctantly, it seemed, both Mekkar and Twofeathers sat. There was no love lost between that pair, Sisko thought. Both of them glared across the table at each other.

"Observe," Zhosh said. He touched the terminal in front of him with one claw, and a holographic map of the Maquis worlds appeared over the center of the table. "This is the disputed territory," the ambassador said, and a section of space took on a pink glow: a long ribbon encompassing perhaps a hundred star systems. "In the greater scheme of things, it is a minor amount of territory to either the Federation or the Cardassian empire. We are proposing that the Federation also cede the following territory." Another ribbon, colored blue and of approximately equal size to the pink territories already marked, appeared alongside the Maquis space. "As you can see, both the Federation and Cardassia would be surrendering equal territory to create this independent buffer state."

Sisko glanced at the Federation ambassadors. No emotions showed on T'Pao's face, but disapproval was plain on Strockman's and DuQuesne's faces. This was a surprise to them, he realized. It had never occurred to them that the Valtusians might ask the Federation to give up yet more territory in the name of peace.

"An interesting idea," Mekkar said loudly, "but one cannot help but wonder what this buffer state would do once its independence is granted. What would stop them from joining the Federation? And what would prevent the Federation from simply annexing them again? No, it seems to me that there are many problems to work out."

"I'm not sure the Federation would be willing to grant additional territory to this buffer state," DuQuesne said. "The problems—"

"Are solvable," Ambassador Zhosh said. "Let us proceed under the assumption that both the Federation and Cardassia are willing to create this buffer state."

"A large assumption," Strockman grumbled.

"But you may proceed," T'Pao said.

Zhosh bowed to her. "The Maquis worlds will gain independence," he went on, "but in return will sign military alliance treaties with both Cardassia and the Federation. If either side attacks or encroaches onto their space, the other side will retaliate. They will be free to trade with both sides. In fact, they will be free . . . period."

"I like it," Twofeathers said softly. "It could work."

Sisko found himself nodding. It just might be the solution to all of their problems, he thought. The Maquis drained resources that were badly needed elsewhere, and the Klingons posed a much bigger threat to Cardassia right now. If the Depta Council, Cardassia's ruling civilian government, could see fit to surrender the territory—and having the Federation surrender a comparable adjacent territory was a stroke of genius—then he saw no obstacle to finally bringing peace to the Maquis worlds.

Julian Bashir trailed Vedek Werron through the bustle of the Promenade. Weaving around a pair of Andorians, darting past a group of Klingons window-shopping at a store selling swords and knives, he kept his target in sight at all times. He felt like a spy shadowing a suspect in one of the holosuite programs he often enjoyed at Quark's. They had been good training for his present mission, he decided. Luckily the Promenade was crowded; he had no trouble ducking out of sight every time Werron paused or glanced around.

He hefted the package he carried inconspicuously under one arm. The real trick would be getting a sample cell from the Vedek without him noticing.

Two Bajorans suddenly joined Werron, and they paused to talk in the middle of the Promenade. Bashir ducked into the nearest doorway—Garak's tailor shop, as it turned out. He almost bumped into Garak in his haste. The Cardassian was just locking the doors.

"Why, Julian," Garak said. "I didn't see you there. Won't you come in?"

"Uh, certainly," Bashir said, peering around the corner. Three more Bajorans had joined Werron, and the six of them were talking animatedly among themselves. What were they saying? He tried to read their lips, but couldn't make out more than a few syllables.

"I just got in a shipment of the most delightful Oslan silks," Garak said. "I hadn't realized word would spread so quickly. That *is* what brings you here on such a fine day, isn't it? And who are those people you're watching?"

"Every day is like any other day on a space station," Bashir said, only half listening. He had to keep his mind on his mission, he reminded himself; Garak might well play a mild-mannered tailor, but he was a veteran of the Obsidian Order. "The environmental controls don't change much, remember?"

"It's a fine day," Garak said expansively, "because I've had a sudden influx of Cardassian customers, all with fresh gossip from home. Business is so good, in fact, that I'm closing early. I'm only going to stay open for paying customers. I believe you said you were interested in a new suit made of Oslan silks?"

"Huh?" What was Garak nattering on about? Bashir forced his attention back to the Cardassian. "A new suit?"

Garak indicated a headless mannequin just inside the door. It had on a gaudy green tunic with large and rather revealing holes sewn in the front and sides. It looked like nothing so much as a gigantic green Swiss cheese, Bashir thought.

"It's perfect for a doctor," Garak said with a smile.

"It's so . . . *revealing*," Bashir said.

"All your patients will see how healthy you are, which in turn will give them greater faith in your medical abilities."

"Uh . . . I'll have to think about it." He leaned forward and glanced up the Promenade. Werron was gazing in his direction. Gulping, Bashir ducked back out of sight. What would a *real* spy do in a situation like this?

Garak folded his arms. "We don't allow loitering in this shop," he said a little sternly. "I'm afraid you're going to have to leave if you're not shopping, Doctor. I *do* want to close up."

"I, uh, just wanted to talk," Bashir said.

"That's different, of course. Perhaps you'd care to join me in Quark's for a drink?"

Bashir risked another glance around the corner. Werron and the other Bajorans were heading into Quark's, he saw. He'd have to follow them, and Garak might provide him with the perfect cover.

"Good idea," he said. "I could use a drink just now."

"Excellent." Garak locked his shop's door, then set off for the bar with Bashir. "What's in the package?" he asked idly, trying to peek in.

Bashir shifted it to his other arm. "A present for my mother," he said.

"It looks heavy."

"Not really."

"Exotic Bajoran spices?" he guessed. "Or Selusian Bakkao?"

Bashir sighed. Would Garak's questions never cease?

"If you must know," he said, "it's really a DNA scanner. It's supposed to be a secret. I'm writing a paper on it."

"If you don't want me prying into your secrets, Doctor," Garak said, grinning a little too widely, "I'll back off. But you can tell me, is it something Quark got for you? Something, perhaps, *Romulan* in origin?"

Bashir sighed. He'd told the truth and Garak still didn't believe him. Well, there wasn't anything he could do about it now.

He led the way into Quark's. This early in the day, the place was only half full. As he gazed about, Bashir saw no sign of last night's brawl. All the tables and chairs had returned to their normal places, and as always patrons sat or stood at the bar or crossed the walkway overhead to the holosuites.

Werron sat at a round table in the center of the

room with the five other Bajorans. As Bashir watched, another Bajoran joined them. They seemed to be earnestly discussing something. Probably plotting to disrupt the negotiations, he thought.

"Your mother wouldn't happen to be visiting the Bajorans at that table, would she?" Garak asked pointedly.

Bashir blushed; he was being too obvious, he realized. He selected a nearby table and sat, dropping the package on the chair next to him.

Rom hurried over. "What can I get you today?" he asked.

"Apple juice," Bashir said.

"Oh, Doctor," Garak said. "One might almost think you were working. Synthale for me, Rom."

"Coming right up," Rom said, and he hurried to the bar.

"What would you do," Bashir asked Garak, "if you needed to get a cell sample from someone without their knowing it? Theoretically, of course," he added hastily. No sense giving anything away, after all.

"Theoretically? And just one cell?"

"That's all I need."

"Hmm." Garak leaned back, considering. "It's not a subject a tailor would know a lot about, of course."

"Of course."

"But I'd say get the Bajoran's glass when he's done with it. He may well leave a skin cell on it. I assume you'd rather do that than break into his quarters and look for stray hair follicles."

"Uh, yes," Bashir said. He glanced over at Werron,

who was drinking something from a large silver goblet. As he watched, the Vedek drained the goblet and called for more. One of the Dabo girls, working the tables as a waitress, hurried to get it for him.

Rom arrived with their drinks.

"Can you do me a favor?" Bashir asked him.

"Yes," Rom said. "And I can get it wholesale, the same as Quark."

Wholesale? Bashir shook his head, suddenly realizing what the Ferengi meant. "Not a new holosuite program," he said. "I want the Vedek's glass from that table over there."

"Vedek Werron?" Rom asked in a loud voice.

Bashir winced. "Keep it down!" he whispered.

"Oh, sorry," Rom said in softer tones. "Do you want to buy it? Or just rent it?"

"Uh, rent it, I guess." He shot Garak a quick glance, but the Cardassian's eyes were on the gambling tables just then.

"I'll put it on your tab." Rom headed for Werron's table.

Bashir watched from the corner of his eye as Rom collected all the empties. Bashir winced a bit as the Ferengi touched the Vedek's goblet. It shouldn't make any difference, he told himself. His scanner could tell Ferengi from Bajoran DNA easily enough. Then to his surprise Rom carried the tray of glasses toward the bar.

Twisting around in his seat, Bashir watched Rom's progress. He dumped all the empties except Werron's into the sanitizer. Calmly, he rinsed and then wiped clean the Vedek's goblet before putting it on a new tray and carrying it triumphantly out to Bashir.

Bashir groaned. "You weren't supposed to wash it!" he said as Rom set it before him.

"You wanted a dirty goblet?" Rom protested. "You never said you wanted a *dirty* goblet!"

"Yes, well, don't worry about it," Bashir said. "Just take it away!"

"What about the fee?"

"You can still add it to my tab."

Scooping up the goblet, Rom hurried off to take another table's order. "Crazy hu-mans!" Bashir heard him muttering.

"So much for that idea," Garak said.

"I have another one, though." Bashir raised his hand and motioned to Rom again, and in a couple of seconds the Ferengi returned.

"What is it this time, Doctor?" Rom asked, bobbing his head nervously. "Another goblet? This one dirty?"

"What are the Bajorans at the Vedek's table drinking?" he asked.

Rom glanced over at Werron and his group. "Bajoran spiced ale," he said.

"Thanks," he said.

Standing, he pulled out his medical tricorder, adjusted the settings to give a contaminated readout of whatever it scanned, and headed for the Vedek's table.

"Excuse me," he said, "but are you drinking Bajoran spiced ale, by any chance? There's been some trouble with it here."

"What kind of trouble?" one of the Bajorans said. He had a half-empty glass in front of him.

"Some slight chance of contamination," Bashir said quickly. "Nothing to be concerned about, of course, if proper precautions are taken—"

Two of the Bajorans leaped to their feet. One grabbed Rom by the front of his shirt and lifted him half a meter off the floor. "What's this about bad ale?" he demanded.

"It's from a replicator!" Rom cried. "It's not bad! There's nothing wrong with it!"

"That's not what my tricorder says," Bashir said, raising it slightly.

"What's all this?" Quark demanded, hurrying over from the bar.

"You're serving bad ale!" another of the Bajorans roared. He shook his fist in Quark's face. "What's the idea, you Ferengi worm?"

"I don't know what you're talking about," Quark snapped back. "Who started this unfounded rumor?"

"Him!" They all pointed at Bashir.

Bashir swallowed and looked around. An unnatural silence had settled over the bar. Everyone in the place had turned to stare at him. He looked at Garak helplessly, but the Cardassian wore an amused expression.

Bashir scanned the nearest goblet of Bajoran spiced ale, then turned the readouts so Quark could see them. They blinked bright red, warning of contamination.

"My tricorder—" Bashir began.

Quark snatched it from his hand. "—is malfunctioning," he said. He gave a nervous laugh as he passed it to Rom.

"It's set wrong," Rom said. He adjusted the controls, scanned the ale again, and passed it to the Bajoran who had been threatening him.

The Bajoran nodded. "There's nothing wrong with it," he admitted.

"False alarm!" Quark shouted so everyone in the room could hear. Bashir glanced around. Everyone seemed to be relaxing again. "Nothing's wrong with the ale! To celebrate, we'll take five percent off the price of all drinks for the next ten minutes!"

People began calling orders to Rom, and Quark hurried back to the bar to fill them. Bashir couldn't miss the dirty look the little Ferengi shot him.

"Thank you for your concern, Doctor," Vedek Werron said. "I appreciate the warning you tried to give."

"Of course," Bashir said. "I'm sorry for the, uh, mistake." He hurried back to his table. His cheeks were burning. If he were a dog, he thought, his tail would be firmly between his legs.

"My plan didn't work," he said to Garak as he slid into his seat. He stared down at his apple juice, brooding on the problem. How was he going to get a cell or a sample of Werron's blood now?

"Don't look," Garak said, "but your Bajorans are leaving the bar."

"What!" Bashir glanced up. Sure enough, the seven of them had risen from their table and begun settling their bill. Perhaps he'd put a scare into them, he thought. Damn it, he'd have to act before they got away. At least Werron brought up the rear.

"May I suggest a more direct approach?" Garak said.

"What do you mean?"

"If it were me, I'd simply walk up to him on some pretext and take a sample of his blood."

"Brilliant," Bashir breathed. The utter simplicity of it all. It could actually work. *Just do it,* part of him said. What could Vedek Werron do after the fact?

"Excuse me," he said, sliding from his seat. He drew a hypo, cut across the room, and reached the door just as Werron was leaving.

He bumped Werron hard from behind, taking his sample from the Bajoran's arm. The hypo made the faintest of hisses.

"Excuse me," Bashir said. "Very sorry, Vedek." He tried to tuck the hypo up his sleeve. Hopefully the Bajoran hadn't felt the tiny, almost unnoticeable little sting from taking the blood sample.

Werron whirled and caught Bashir's hand.

"What by the Prophets do you think you're doing?" he demanded. "What did you just inject me with, Doctor?"

"Inject . . . no, I took a sample of blood!" Bashir said. He'd put his foot in it now, he realized. The Vedek thought he was trying to assassinate him.

"Why?" Werron demanded, eyes hard.

"Uh . . . testing for Xolon poisoning?" Bashir suggested. He held the hypo up and swirled it gently. The blood inside remained a dark red which meant Werron wasn't a changeling. *I was so sure,* he thought.

He met the Vedek's gaze. Rage had contorted Werron's face, and those piercing green eyes seemed to bore into Bashir.

"What's wrong?" the other Bajorans were saying, gathering around the Vedek.

"He," Werron said, pointing, "stabbed me with a needle and took a sample of my blood!"

"There are no needles in hyposprays," Bashir said, swallowing frantically. He began to back into the bar and suddenly found himself trodding on toes.

"What's going on?" another Bajoran voice asked. "Vedek? Are you all right?"

"No," Werron said.

Strong hands seized Bashir's arms from behind. Bashir tried to wrench free, but couldn't. The circle around him was closing in. Gulping, he felt a surge of panic. He should have known better than to listen to Garak's mad plan. How was he going to get out of this?

CHAPTER
19

WATCHING FROM THE safety of her locker, Kira didn't know what to do. Odo's presence complicated things. Worst of all, he appeared to be cooperating completely with the changeling and the Jem'Hadar. Had he gone over to the other side? They'd only been apart for a day. She didn't think so, but it had to remain a possibility. It might explain the hunt for them in the access corridors.

No sense getting paranoid, she told herself. *Snoct said those hunts happened all the time. Our presence is just a coincidence.*

Finally she decided to trust her instincts. Odo had always been a friend. He wouldn't betray them.

The ship's engines powered up, and she felt them lift from the landing bay's deck. She watched the Jem'Hadar pilots bring them around, then fly out, passing through the series of force fields that served as the giant landing bay's airlock. Then they were outside, and as soon as they were a safe distance out, they went to warp. She saw stars streaking past on the forward viewscreen.

Odo continued to stand in front with the changeling and the Jem'Hadar pilots. He was chatting with them, but she couldn't make out the words. If only he'd face her for a minute.

Finally he turned. None of the others were looking—this was her chance.

Opening the locker, she leaned out and waved. He must have seen her, she thought, but he gave no sign of it. Which meant he hadn't betrayed them.

A few minutes later, he wandered toward the back of the ship with the other changeling.

"This is an interesting vessel," she heard him saying. "I've never seen anything like it. What kind is it?"

"The first of the new Jakar-class," the changeling said. "It's a prototype from the shipyards in orbit around Octyne III. We'll stop there, if you like."

"If you don't mind, I would like to examine the engines more closely."

The changeling gestured magnanimously. "Of course, Odo. Your own people have no secrets from you."

"I'm sure," Odo said dryly. Turning, he headed into the aft compartment. Kira watched through the ventilation slits in the storage compartment. Fortunately, the other changeling didn't follow.

Odo approached the warp engines. He seemed completely fascinated by them, Kira thought, studying them like an engineer on an inspection circuit.

Finally Kira decided he was close enough to risk trying to talk with him. She pressed her lips close to the air vents and whispered, "Odo, it's me, Kira."

"I saw you," he whispered back. "Is Worf aboard, too?"

"Yes," she said. "When are we going to land on Daborat V?"

"It's our second stop," Odo said, "after the energy conversion complex at Skovar VI. Have patience. I'll do the best I can to get you out safely when we reach the planet."

"All right," Kira said.

She sank back as Odo, finishing his inspection, returned to the front of the ship. This was going to be a long journey, she thought. Already her muscles were starting to tense up a bit from being in such a confined space. She shifted uncomfortably. It had to be ten times worse for Worf because of his size. She just hoped he and Snoct Sneyd could hold out until they made planetfall. Still, perhaps they'd have a chance to stretch when they landed on Skovar VI.

Kira spent the next few hours dozing, trying to make the time pass more quickly. When the tenor of the engines changed suddenly, though, she snapped awake. Something had happened, she realized.

She lowered her head and peered out the air vents.

Through the forward viewports she could just make out a planet. They must have arrived, she realized.

She twisted a little, trying to relieve her aching muscles, and bumped the locker's door hard with her left knee. The thump sounded loud in the confined space, but neither the Jem'Hadar nor the changeling turned around.

They entered the atmosphere. It was a class-M planet, Kira rapidly realized, as they pierced the dense layer of clouds covering the surface and towering green forests appeared.

When buildings appeared on the horizon, they landed smoothly, and the side hatch popped open. She heard the ramp extending to the ground outside.

A sudden banging sound close by startled her. Worf? No, she realized, as Snoct Sneyd burst into view, it was the little alien. He made a mad dash for the hatch.

One of the Jem'Hadar leaped forward and seized Snoct by the back of the neck. Snoct whipped around and tried to sink his fangs into the warrior's arm, but the Jem'Hadar hit him twice with a rocklike fist. Snoct sagged a little, hissing.

"What is this creature?" the changeling asked.

"An Iffalian," said one of the pilots. He told briefly how the little alien had sneaked onto their ship. "We have been hunting it for several months for sport," he concluded.

"Dispose of it," said the changeling.

The Jem'Hadar holding Snoct reached down and drew his sidearm.

When Snoct Sneyd let out a plaintive whimper, the breath caught in Kira's throat. How could the changeling order a murder so callously? Snoct was sentient. They couldn't just shoot him.

Instinctively she reached for her phaser. She wasn't going to sit here while someone she knew was butchered. Not when she could do something about it.

"Wait!" cried Odo, gazing from the changeling to Snoct Sneyd. "You can't kill an intelligent creature like that!"

Kira relaxed a little. Maybe she wouldn't have to act, she thought.

"Intelligent?" the changeling said with a sneer. "A truly intelligent being would have escaped long ago. No, Odo, you need to learn how we do things in the Gamma Quadrant." He nodded to the Jem'Hadar. "Proceed."

The Jem'Hadar raised their weapons to fire.

Time to act. Kira burst from her locker, phaser firing. She liked the little fellow too much to stand by and let him be executed.

CHAPTER
20

AS THE CIRCLE of angry Bajorans closed around him, Bashir realized he only had one defense—the truth.

"I needed a sample of your blood," he blurted out to Werron, "to verify that you were not a changeling infiltrating the station from the Gamma Quadrant." He held up the vial. "You've just been cleared; you're Bajoran."

Werron paused and held up one hand for the vial. Bashir felt a quick wave of relief as the Vedek's followers released him. He handed the vial over.

"I fail to understand," Werron said slowly, staring at his blood, "why you'd think I might be a changeling infiltrator."

"You appeared suddenly a year ago as a public figure after twenty years of near invisibility."

"It was the will of the Prophets."

"And then there were your attacks on Gul Mekkar—"

Werron's face twisted with rage. "Those are righteous attacks! He is the Butcher of Belmast! We must be avenged!"

"That may be," Bashir said quickly. No sense upsetting him more. "But we think the changelings want this conference stopped. What better way than to have one of the chief negotiators removed?"

"A better way," Werron said, "would be to infiltrate one of the negotiating teams."

"We already thought of that," Bashir said.

"It all makes sense," Werron said slowly. He turned to his followers, and Bashir thought he saw a vengeful gleam in the Vedek's eye as he loudly announced, "The Cardassian war criminal Gul Mekkar, the Butcher of Belmast, is a changeling!"

"But I tested Mekkar's blood!" Bashir protested from behind him. There wasn't any possibility of the Cardassian being a changeling.

"But," said Werron, turning back to him, "is there any way to tell if the results might have somehow been faked? Can you say in all certainty that he couldn't have found some way around your little test?"

Bashir drew himself up. "I designed the DNA scanner myself," he said. "I tested everyone in the Cardassian delegation. They all passed. Just as the Valtusians, the Maquis, and the Federation ambassadors passed."

"But couldn't they have found a way to fool your

screening method?" Werron prodded. "Couldn't they have found some trick to get around it?"

Bashir hesitated. He couldn't think of a way, but that didn't mean one didn't exist . . . did it? Even if it was a slender possibility.

"Perhaps," he admitted.

Werron smiled serenely. "That," he said, "is all I wanted to know."

Benjamin Sisko sighed. He wished he could cover his ears to shut out the noise, but he knew everyone in the room—Cardassians, Humans, and Valtusians alike—would take affront at the gesture. He wanted them united but not united against him.

"Paragraph one, subsection three," Gul Mekkar said in a loud voice and for the fourth time, "remains utterly unacceptable."

They were going through the Valtusian peace proposal line by line now, arguing over language, interpretation, and consequences. In short, they were bickering.

"I suppose you'd like to simply clear out all the human settlers," the Maquis representative said with a sneer. "Just ship us off to work camps, like you did with Bajoran troublemakers, while you rape our worlds, too!"

"Bajor got what it deserved!" Mekkar roared, placing his fists on the table and half rising from his seat. "The only way to deal with terrorists is with total, ruthless, merciless force! The old ways handled troublemakers just fine!"

Sisko leaped to his feet. "Enough!" he cried. He had never seen such a pack of spoiled children. "Let's take a half hour break to cool our heads. This meeting is recessed."

Sisko stalked from the room. He wanted to pound the walls with his fists. Of all the obstructionist, petty, and stupid things that had been going on throughout these negotiations, Gul Mekkar's latest demands took top prize. How could he even *hope* for peace with such inflexible demands? And the Federation negotiators weren't much better.

He turned and headed for the turbolift. An hour . . . it wouldn't be nearly enough time, he thought, for them to get over their petty, demanding ways. At this rate, it would take years to settle the Maquis problem.

The turbolift doors opened; he got in. "Ops," he said.

He rode in silence, reflecting on everything that had happened. Hopefully Kira, Worf, and Odo were having better luck, he thought. If their mission succeeded, the urgency of settling the Maquis problem would be over, and then the Cardassians could stop trying to use it as an edge in the negotiating process.

When the lift doors opened, he stepped out and surveyed Ops with an experienced eye. Everything seemed normal here, he thought. All the stations were manned, and nobody seemed to be running around in a panic. He nodded. At least he could count on his people to keep things running in times like these, when he was too occupied to keep up on DS9's day-by-day operations.

Dax spotted him and hurried over. She had a half smile on her face that Sisko recognized as trouble. He gave an inward groan. What now?

"What is it, Dax?" he asked. "Riots on the Promenade? Bajoran terrorists threatening to blow up Gul Mekkar and his delegation?"

"Worse," she said. "Vedek Werron and Dr. Bashir are waiting for you in your office."

It was, Sisko decided, one of those days where nothing went right. He'd hoped to avoid meeting with Werron; his fanatical politics went beyond even Kai Winn's.

"Thanks," he said. "Any other bad news?"

"No," she said with another smile. "But I'll let you know."

Shaking his head, he headed for his office. As the door opened, he found Bashir perched on the corner of his desk talking to Werron, who sat in one of the two chairs. Bashir leaped to his feet, looking guilty. Good, Sisko thought, but he didn't let that show.

"It's nice to meet with you again, Vedek Werron," Sisko said, nodding politely to the Bajoran.

"I feel the same way, Emissary," Werron said.

"I am afraid I have a very hectic schedule. I am still looking into Gul Mekkar's history, so I have nothing to report on that front, if that's why you're here."

"It's not," Werron said.

Sisko nodded. He'd suspected as much. "Very well," he said. "I can only spare you a few minutes, however. Do you mind if we dispense with formalities and come right to the point?"

Werron frowned a little, and for a second Sisko thought he might have offended him. But then Werron too nodded.

"I think that may be best," he said.

Sisko listened intently as Werron argued that Mekkar must be a changeling infiltrator. Sisko didn't believe it for an instant himself, considering how all the ambassadors had passed Bashir's surprise DNA scans, but he allowed himself to accept the idea for an instant. If Mekkar had been replaced, might that not explain his constant delays and incessant demands? Several times now they had almost thrown the negotiations off track.

"It occurred to me," Bashir said, "that one or more of the ambassadors might have been replaced *after* we scanned them."

"They've been under such close supervision," Sisko began, shaking his head, "that I find the possibility difficult to believe."

"Then explain this to me," Werron said. "Why would a notorious war criminal like Mekkar return to Bajoran space? The *real* Mekkar would never have dared such a thing. The *real* Mekkar would have known we would find some way to bring him to justice."

That argument did make a certain amount of sense, Sisko thought. He reflected for a moment on the possibility and had to admit that, remote as it seemed, it still worried him. He frowned. Perhaps he could turn it to his advantage, though. Werron seemed determined that Gul Mekkar had to be guilty of *something*.

"You're certain he is a changeling?" Sisko said.

"Yes," Werron said firmly. "I would stake my reputation on it."

"You just have," Sisko finally said. "We will test Gul Mekkar. However," he added, "if Mekkar and the other Cardassian delegates turn out to be real Cardassians, I will ask you and your followers to leave the station until the negotiations are over."

"And if they're changelings?" Werron demanded.

"If they're changelings, you'll be a hero," Sisko said. Playing to a Vedek's vanity had often worked for him in the past. "You'll be the one who uncovered the plot, when all of Starfleet couldn't."

Werron mulled that over. "Agreed," he finally said.

Sisko rose. "Very well. If you'll leave Dr. Bashir with me to make the arrangements, we'll contact you as soon as we're ready to begin. You do, I trust, want to be present when the tests are carried out."

"Yes." Werron turned and strode purposefully from the room. Sisko thought he detected a bit of a strut in the Bajoran's walk.

"Are you sure this is a good idea?" Bashir asked as soon as they were alone.

"You tell me, Doctor," Sisko said. "You brought Werron here, remember?"

Bashir sighed and shook his head a little ruefully. "He had me half believing Gul Mekkar had somehow slipped past my DNA scan," he admitted. "I kept trying to picture ways the delegates might have fooled my equipment."

"And did they?" Sisko asked. He wanted to know the truth, no matter how painful to Bashir.

"I just don't know anymore," the doctor said with a helpless shrug. "Are you really going to test Mekkar again? Singling him out may simply enrage him further."

"I realize that. Which is why I intend to test *all* the delegates again." Sisko leaned back. "And this time," he went on, "you're going to take blood tests as well as DNA tests, just to make certain. And when none of them turns out to be a changeling, I'll have Werron— and all the other Bajoran troublemakers—off this station for the duration of the peace conference, which will be a load off of everyone's mind."

CHAPTER
21

WORF BURST FROM his locker the moment he heard the changeling give the order for Snoct's execution. Blood roaring in his ears, he dove forward, phaser firing.

Some distant and more primitive part of him thought, this was what a Klingon lived for, the *may'boq*—the battle fever that came with fighting. It sent his emotions soaring and filled his body with an almost electric energy.

His first shot hit the Jem'Hadar holding Snoct by the back of the neck.

The universe seemed to be slowing down around him, Worf thought. He felt the thudding rhythm of his heart pumping blood in his chest. Colors blared with vibrant energy as his sight narrowed to the targets ahead of him.

He fired his phaser a second time, jagging to the side. The second Jem'Hadar warrior began to crumple. Then Worf fired at the copilot, who dodged, drawing his own weapon. As the pilot started to aim, Worf dove toward the floor. If he could get under his guard long enough to fire a second shot . . .

The changeling began to shimmer with a strange golden light, body rippling like wind on a lake. He was shape-shifting, Worf realized. He hesitated a fraction of an instant, torn between two targets. *Go for the Jem'Hadar,* a voice inside him said.

A phaser blast from behind Worf struck the copilot in the chest, throwing him back against the bulkhead with a thud. That shot had come from Kira, Worf realized.

Worf turned his dive into a forward roll, coming up in a kneeling position. He snapped off his third shot, striking the changeling, but it didn't seem to have any effect. He would be a more difficult target, Worf realized, climbing to his feet.

The changeling returned to humanoid form and folded his arms. He regarded Worf with an expression of intense curiosity.

"A Klingon," he heard it murmur. "Superb."

The *may'boq* began to pass, and the room dropped back into normal focus again. Worf frowned, trying to think. It was hard after the battle fever. He still heard a faint murmur of blood in his ears, and it left him charged for combat.

"Thank you!" Snoct Sneyd called in a shrill voice. "Good friends!"

"Idiot," Kira snapped at the little alien. She stalked forward and pushed the pilot's body out of the way, then slid into his seat. Worf kept his phaser trained on the changeling, covering her. She began taking readings off the instruments.

The changeling didn't seem to be making any hostile moves, so Worf took a final cleansing breath and walked forward as normally as he could. It felt good to have stretched his battle muscles, but the changeling represented a huge problem for him. What would Captain Picard have done? Better still, what would Captain Sisko do?

Delegate, he thought with a mental cry of triumph. Both captains had different strengths, but one trait they shared was the ability to let others pitch in and help.

"Odo," Worf said, "what do you recommend we do with the prisoners?"

"There's only one who matters," Odo said, looking at the changeling next to him.

"Then you have learned something from our time together," the changeling said smoothly. "There are only two of them, Odo. Help me capture them. The Alpha Quadrant can be yours, too."

The changeling began to shapeshift, and Worf snapped up his phaser, thumbing the controls to a lethal setting. Would it be enough?

Then Odo stepped between them.

"No," he said to the changeling. "I have rejected all you stand for. These are my friends. I won't betray them."

The changeling slowly returned to his normal humanoid form. "You are still young, Odo, but you will only have so many chances to rejoin your people."

"I've made my decision," Odo said firmly.

"Perhaps you will regret it." Worf thought he heard a note of disapproval mixed with disappointment in that smooth, alien voice. "No *true* changeling has ever harmed another. I will not fight you over two *solids*. You are truly not one of us, Odo. Perhaps something will be done about that."

Odo seemed to relax a little. "You will not be injured," Odo promised.

"Unless you try to fight or escape," Worf added. No sense making their intentions unclear, he thought. Odo might have qualms about hurting a fellow changeling, but he didn't. He was more than ready to meet any danger this one posed.

The changeling inclined his head slightly. "Then I will rest." He swirled into a new shape, a gracefully sculpted mound with the faintest hint of head and arms, and solidified in that form.

Worf stared at him distrustfully for a second. How could you guard against something like that sneaking up on you? You couldn't, he realized. He'd have to rely on Odo to keep the changeling under control.

But that still left the three unconscious Jem'Hadar to worry about. They, at least, offered no real threat at the moment. But they would be regaining consciousness soon, and he wanted to be ready.

"I have cord in my pack," he said to Snoct Sneyd. "Get it and we will tie them up."

"Gladly!" the little alien said. It scampered to the back of the shuttle on all fours.

Worf seized the first Jem'Hadar he'd shot and dragged him into the middle section of the ship. In a moment Snoct Sneyd rejoined him with a coil of light rope. Worf drew his knife, cut a length, and began binding the warrior's hands behind his back.

Kira lifted the ship from the spaceport and headed east at top speed. They couldn't very well take the Jem'Hadar or the changeling with them to Daborat V, she thought, so they'd have to dump them somewhere out of the way.

Calling up the planetary survey on the ship's computer, she studied the information. The colonization of Skovar IV hadn't been completed, she saw; the large southern continent on the other side of the planet hadn't been settled yet. That should do nicely. What better place to leave them? The changeling would, of course, make it back to civilization in less than a week. All he had to do was turn into a fish and swim or a bird and fly. But that would give them all the time they needed to get to Daborat V and finish their mission.

She punched in the destination coordinates and activated the autopilot. Now, she thought, rising and heading aft, to see about helping Worf . . .

Half an hour later, the great southern continent came up below them. Kira took back control and slowed the ship, scanning the shoreline for a suitable landing place. She didn't see one. Huge waves pounded against jagged black rocks, and tall obsidian cliffs topped by dense jungle rose from the ocean.

Well, nobody said stranding captives had to be easy, she thought. She headed inland, over the lush, verdant green jungle filled with exotic life-forms. Birdlike animals with bright red and yellow wings flitted among the trees, and she could see several enormous creatures with six legs crashing about, their bulbous red heads jutting above the tops of the trees as they nibbled leaves from upper branches. They reminded her for an instant of the extinct giant reptiles of Bajor's past.

The jungle wouldn't be a safe place to leave their prisoners, she decided, so on she flew until the jungles gave way to sprawling yellowish green grasslands threaded by blue streams and rivers. More leathery-winged birds flapped out of the way as she brought the ship down, and smaller reptiles with six legs bounded away in herds.

"This is it," she called back. "We'll leave them here."

Abruptly the changeling shifted into his humanoid form. He stared out the viewport, then looked at Kira. She felt uncomfortable under his gaze, as though he were dissecting her with his eyes.

"This is little more than an inconvenience to me," he said.

"I know," Kira answered, "but it's better than killing you, which is the alternative."

He smiled thinly. "I don't think you could do that."

"Unlike Starfleet officers, I have no qualms about killing when it's necessary."

"I don't doubt your ethics," he said in a voice that chilled her. "I doubt your ability." Turning, he strode quickly into the passenger compartment. Odo followed, and after a second's hesitation, Kira did, too. Somehow, she believed the changeling. She'd seen enough people try to kill Odo over the years. What must a fully mature changeling be capable of?

Snoct and Worf were carrying the unconscious Jem'Hadar down the ramp and laying them out on the grass. The changeling stood nearby, watching without a trace of emotion. He might have been supervising the unloading of bags of grain, for all he cared, Kira thought.

"Auron," Odo said. "Will you be all right?"

He sneered a little. "Of course. Nothing here can harm me."

Odo nodded once. When they had off-loaded the last Jem'Hadar, Worf and Snoct returned to the ship. Kira followed, then lastly Odo. He didn't like stranding the other changeling here, she realized as she closed and sealed the hatch.

"Don't worry about him," she said.

"I'm not."

Kira returned to her seat, strapped herself in, took the controls, and lifted off smoothly. She circled around once to see what the changeling—Auron, Odo had called him—would do. She could see him staring up at her, with the three Jem'Hadar lying on the ground just behind him.

Suddenly he changed form, becoming a huge winged beast. He flapped his leathery wings until he caught an updraft, then soared high into the sky. Banking, he headed east for the other continent and civilization.

The least he could have done was untie the Jem'Hadar first, Kira thought. Knowing them, they would doubtless be able to work their way free in a few hours, but nonetheless, it showed how little he thought of "solids," as they called other life-forms. They were disposable in his philosophy.

She shook her head. Not her problem now. They still had their mission to finish.

She punched in the course for Daborat V, and as they left the planet's gravitational field, they went to warp.

Twelve hours later, they entered the Daborat V system. Kira shut off the autopilot and resumed manual control.

The planet grew rapidly in the viewport. It looked like a beautiful class-M world, with deep blue oceans, three major land masses, and large polar ice caps. White clouds dotted the atmosphere. Bajor, she thought, would look like this again someday.

A second later, a light series of tones sounded. "Daborat V spaceport control to unidentified ship," a voice said. "Please identify."

"Odo!" she called.

He jogged into the cockpit. "What is it, Major?"

"They're hailing us."

"Put them on. I'll take care of it."

"I sure hope this works," she muttered to herself. They had almost literally bet everything on Odo's being able to get them past the security checkpoints. If not, they would have to run, come back later, and try to sneak a landing.

She activated the viewscreen, and a Jem'Hadar warrior in a black uniform different from the others she'd seen appeared. Probably a local official, she thought.

He took one look at Odo and saluted. "Founder!" he said.

Odo leveled his gaze at the officer. "I want clearance to land," he said in his most authoritative voice. Kira glanced sideways at him. She'd heard that same overbearing tone in the changeling whom they'd stranded on Skovar IV.

"Immediately." The officer punched something into his console, then gave landing coordinates.

Odo nodded, then severed the connection.

"That was easy," Kira said.

"Too easy," Worf said. He had come up behind them while they were getting landing clearance. Now he glowered a bit at Odo. "Almost as if they were expecting us."

"Are you implying that this is a trap?" Odo demanded.

"I am not implying anything," Worf said. "It seemed too easy to me."

Kira sighed and leaned back in her seat. Odo and Worf had been working at odds with one another almost since they'd met, it sometimes seemed. The Klingon didn't know Odo as well as she knew him, she told herself. At first he always seemed a little off-putting, but now that she knew his quirks, she would have trusted him with her life. On this mission, in fact, she already had.

"I'm willing to take this at face value," she said to Worf.

"Thank you, Major," Odo said.

"Now let's get back to business at hand, shall we?" She turned back to the controls and locked in the landing coordinates she'd been given, activating the autopilot. The ship nosed down and began its descent.

A bit of turbulence shook the ship suddenly. It was always a little bumpy when you entered a planet's atmosphere, she knew, so that didn't worry her. Odo steadied himself against the back of her chair, and Worf slid into the copilot's seat.

The planet grew before them. Kira stared at the huge landing field now appearing through the clouds below. It was immense, she realized, easily twice the size of the largest city on Bajor. Hundreds if not thousands of ships were parked here, ranging in size from tiny starships like their own to behemoths nearly as big as the *Enterprise* had been.

A series of bleeps greeted them.

"We're being hailed," Worf said beside her. "It's ground control. They want us to slave the controls over to them. Major?"

"I'm taking care of it." She didn't like losing control of the ship, but she didn't see any alternative.

She didn't want to attract attention to herself by refusing what might well be a routine landing procedure here. As she activated the automatic landing sequencers, the ship's controls suddenly locked her out.

She slid from her chair as the turbulence eased, using the break to check her phaser and personal cloaker. You could never be too careful, she thought. Everything seemed in working order. Now that they'd reached Daborat V and the end was in sight, they'd have to move quickly to make up for lost time. Worf too was checking his weapons, she noted. Odo merely stood with his arms folded, watching out the front viewport as they passed over hundreds of parked ships.

Snoct began making a happy chittering sound from the passenger cabin. At least one of us is home, she thought.

They angled down toward a less crowded area of the landing field, approaching an open spot between two small Jem'Hadar fighter ships. The shuttle slowed, moved to one side, then settled to the ground. Kira felt a slight bump when they touched down, then the engines powered down. The sudden silence was deafening.

Odo strode to the hatch. Kira drew here weapon and followed him. After a second's hesitation, Worf did the same. The hatch popped open, admitting a stale, dry breeze scented with machine oils, exhaust fumes, and sun-baked duracrete, and the ramp telescoped down to the pavement.

Kira went first, then Odo, then Worf. The landing field looked deserted: no signs of people at all, just parked ships in all directions. Everyone had probably gone to the city proper on leave. She clipped the phaser back onto her belt.

Worf turned in a complete circle as he reached the pavement, taking everything in, then put away his own phaser. He seemed almost disappointed in their reception, Kira thought.

"A hundred million thanks," Snoct said, bounding out the open hatch excitedly. "I am home! I am home!"

Kira told him, "We're glad to have helped."

"If I can ever be of service, let me know," he promised. "Just ask any of the maintenance people at the spaceport for Snoct Sneyd. They all know me!"

"There is one more small thing you can do right now," Odo said.

"Name it!" Snoct said.

"We need directions."

That's right, Kira thought. Leave it to Odo to remember.

"We're looking for a bar called the Empty Coffin," she said. "Do you know it?"

Snoct shuddered. "A horrible place," he said. "It's in Old Town. The scum of Daborat V go there. Stay away, stay away!"

"We cannot," Worf said. "We need to meet someone there."

Snoct shuddered again. "Then yes, I know how to get there." He pointed down a row of shuttlecraft.

"Go that way. When the landing field ends, you will see the city. Look for a small, filthy street named Jork's End. That's where you will find the Empty Coffin."

"How will we know it?"

"It's the only bar there."

"Thank you," Kira said.

"Happy to help!" Snoct said. Then, dropping to all fours, he dashed in the opposite direction.

At least some good had come of the mission so far, Kira thought. They'd rescued one small alien and brought him home. She drew herself up and took a deep breath. Now to see about rescuing Orvor and retrieving the retrovirus.

They set out down the row of spaceships. Once a pair of ground vehicles glided silently past, suspended a few centimeters off the ground by antigravity skids, and though a few Jem'Hadar troops sat aboard, they didn't slow down for a second. Kira forced herself to untense. It really did seem as though Odo's presence guaranteed them free passage throughout the Dominion, she reflected.

Still they walked, and it began to grow dark. Finally, as dusk swept across the spaceport, huge lights came on, flooding the duracrete pavement with a harsh white illumination.

Fifteen minutes later they came to the edge of the spaceport. The duracrete simply ended and the city itself began. Here, this close to the landing field, the buildings appeared small, dark, and run-down looking. The street lamps had all been smashed, and the only illumination was a grayish glow spilling over from the spaceport. Empty doors and windows gaped like the eye sockets of alien skulls, Kira thought with a shiver.

This couldn't be the best neighborhood, she realized, glancing around uneasily. It was exactly the sort of place she'd expect to find a dive called the Empty Coffin. No wonder Snoct Sneyd had warned them to stay away.

Sudden scuttling movement caught her eye. She whirled, phaser ready.

"Worf . . ." she began.

"I saw it." He drew his own phaser, squinting into the dark. "A figure—"

"Just a homeless scavenger of some kind, I'm sure," Odo said. "This way." He started up the street, taking the lead, and Kira followed. Now, as they walked, she saw furtive movements all around them in the dark. She longed for a torch of some sort. Light would have made her feel safer.

The buildings began to grow larger and better kept. A few now had doors and windows, she noticed, and finally they came to a series of working street lamps. A scattering of humanoids—some with tall, narrow skulls, some with broad lumpy faces, all dressed in what looked like worn black animal leather—lounged beneath the lights, watching them. Their eyes were hungry, she thought. Ahead, a scattering of buildings glowed with light.

Odo strode up to one of the aliens without a

moment's hesitation. "I'm looking for the Empty Coffin," he announced.

The alien—bipedal, humanoid, but with a head that was almost completely flat on top—grunted once, then pulled a knife.

"Money," he said.

Odo's left arm suddenly extended an extra meter, wrapping around the alien's knife hand. Odo squeezed, and Kira heard the pop of joints dislocating. The knife clattered on the ground, and the alien began to whimper.

"I'm looking for the Empty Coffin," Odo repeated.

With its one good hand, the alien pointed up the street.

"Thank you," Odo said, and he continued on.

Kira caught up with him. "Why did you do that?" she demanded.

"To show we weren't afraid of them," he said. "We are being followed—no, don't look back—and I want them to know we're not going to be easy prey."

Kira swallowed. She'd been watching everything around them carefully, but couldn't see anyone following them. Odo had keener senses than she did, she reminded herself, plus he had security training. Dropping back half a meter, she matched Worf's stride.

"Do you see them?" she said.

"Yes," he said warily. "I counted fifteen."

Then, ahead, she spotted a building that glowed with soft pastel lights. There were flickering neon signs in front, she saw, written in the local dialect.

Unfortunately, she couldn't read them, but she recognized the blinking coffin shape over the door. This had to be the bar they were looking for.

Odo held back, looking into the darkness, as she went up the worn steps to the front door. It slid aside soundlessly for her. Taking a deep breath, she stepped in and surveyed the room.

A long bar stretched across the back, and aliens of various sizes and descriptions lounged there sipping drinks. Booths lined the walls to her left and right, and a handful of tables sat in the middle of the room. Weird atonal music came from hidden speakers in the corners. As she'd expected, there were no Jem'Hadar present.

Every eye in the place had focused on her. The people standing at the bar turned to face her. Several of them began picking their teeth with long, rapierlike knives.

Worf and Odo entered behind her. As they stepped in, every being in the room suddenly whipped out disruptors. She surveyed the alien faces and found emotions ranging from anger to outrage to disgust.

"Hands up!" the bartender sneered, coming out from around the bar. His piggish gray snout curled back to reveal a mouth full of needle-sharp teeth. He held a huge disruptor rifle in his four arms.

"Better do as he says," Odo murmured.

Dismayed, Kira raised her arms over her head. Behind her, she sensed Odo and Worf doing the same. This rescue, she thought, was not going very well.

CHAPTER
22

GLANCING AT WERRON, Bashir, and the four security guards, Sisko stepped up to the conference room door. This wasn't going to be pretty, he knew. He punched his access code into the hand pad. All the ambassadors had given them so much trouble over the initial DNA scans, he could only imagine their reaction when he asked for actual blood samples.

Bashir looked as nervous as Sisko felt. The doctor had his arms full with the DNA scanner, medical tricorder, hypo, and a small case of glass vials. Each of the eleven ambassadors *would* have his or her own sample neatly taken, labeled, and set in the center of the conference room table. This time there would be no mistakes, no possibilities of an error, and no question of changeling subterfuge.

"Ready, Doctor?" he asked, keying in the final digit.

Bashir nodded, all business now. It was nice to see how he had matured into his post, Sisko reflected. Three years ago, he thought, Bashir would have giggled nervously and made a joke.

"Then let's do it," Sisko said.

The door whisked open. He'd timed their arrival perfectly, and sure enough everyone else already sat in their seats. His gaze swept across the round table, taking in the Valtusians, the Federation negotiators, the Cardassians, and lastly the two Maquis.

Their argument had broken off the second the door whisked open. They stared in surprise at him.

"May I have your attention, please," he began in a loud voice. "Thanks to Vedek Werron, we have reason to believe that the changelings have indeed managed to infiltrate this conference."

"We already passed your screening tests," Gul Mekkar said in a gravely voice.

"For security reasons, we must administer new tests. To make sure there is no question of faking the results, we will also draw blood samples. No one will be exempted, including myself. Doctor?"

"Put your hand here," Bashir said, offering his scanner.

Sisko did so. It promptly announced he was human.

"Now the blood test, Doctor," Sisko said. Keeping his gaze locked with Mekkar's, he rolled up his sleeve and offered his arm to Bashir. He felt a brief cold prickling sensation, then a second later Bashir released him.

"We'll know in a second," Bashir said.

Sisko glanced over. The doctor held a small vial up to the light, swirling it gently in a counterclockwise direction. The deep crimson blood in the container remained unchanged.

"He's human," Bashir announced.

"The process," Sisko went on, "only requires a few seconds. I trust you will all cooperate so we may proceed with the more important business at hand."

"If not . . .?" Mekkar demanded.

"You will be detained in a cell for the next twenty-four hours, under close observation. Periodically, changelings must revert to a liquid state. If you remain unchanged after twenty-four hours, you will be released to resume your negotiations. However," and Sisko let his voice drop an octave, "I trust that detention will not be necessary."

"This is preposterous—" Mekkar began.

"We will begin," Sisko went on, ignoring him, "with the Federation negotiators."

DuQuesne leaped to his feet. "Absurd!" he cried. "You can't do this! It violates every civil right we've won over the last six centuries!"

"Be quiet," T'Pao said. She rose and circled the table to where Bashir waited. "I will go first. In matters of security, there can be no politics. Remember the conference on Earth with the Romulans."

She placed her hand on the DNA scanner.

"Subject is Vulcan," it announced.

Next T'Pao bared her arm. Bashir drew a sample of her green blood, swirled it, held it up to the light.

"She's Vulcan," he said.

"Logically," she said, "we are all interested in peace. Why not permit this painless examination, which will then allow us to continue with our work, rather than waste more precious time?" Leave it to a Vulcan to cut through the red tape, Sisko thought. T'Pao reclaimed her seat. "You are next, Ambassador," she said to DuQuesne.

His face revealed his anger. "Very well," he said with ill-concealed fury. He circled the table, rolling up his sleeve for Dr. Bashir.

"Human," both the DNA scanner and Bashir said.

"Hah," DuQuesne said to Sisko. Sulkily, he sat next to T'Pao again, folding his arms and glaring.

Strockman went next. Bashir quickly pronounced him human as well.

"As we already knew," DuQuesne said. "This is a waste of time, and I promise you," he said pointedly to Sisko, "that formal complaints will be lodged against you for this outrage. We didn't come here for daily blood tests, and you've interrupted our negotiations at a critical juncture."

"That's a risk I'm willing to take," Sisko said. After everything that had happened so far, he knew Admiral Dulev would back him. He nodded to Bashir. "The Maquis ambassadors next, if you please, Doctor."

Ambassador Twofeathers went first and passed, as

did Ambassador Kravits. Sisko nodded; he'd expected no less. Now would come the real test.

"Now the Cardassians, if you please."

"I feel the same way your own negotiating team does," Gul Mekkar said, rising. "However, I bow to the inevitable. Begin your tests, Doctor."

Mekkar placed his hand on the scanner. Sisko leaned forward in anticipation.

"Subject DNA passes," the scanner announced. "Subject is Cardassian."

Sisko relaxed even as Bashir took Mekkar's blood sample. *He isn't a changeling. Now I can be rid of Werron once and for all.* At least something good had come of it, he thought.

He glanced over at Vedek Werron, who had watched all this impassively. The Vedek's face showed not a flicker of emotion. Nevertheless Sisko knew it had to hurt. He'd staked his reputation on it, after all, and now he'd be deported from DS9 like a common troublemaker. *I'm sure he'll manage to put a good spin on it, though,* Sisko thought. *He'll just declare his mission a success and leave. That'll be the end of it.*

Only the Valtusians remained, but testing was little more than a formality. The whole conference had been their idea, after all, and they had been the ones working toward peace.

"Now the Valtusian ambassadors," he said.

Ambassador Zhosh and the others rose. But rather than argue as Sisko expected, Zhosh removed a small tube from a hidden pocket in his robes, twisted it once, and suddenly the hum of a transporter beam filled the room.

Sisko whirled. "Stop them!" he cried to the guards.

It was too late, he realized a millisecond later. They were already dematerializing. In the transporter beam, he saw them starting to shimmer and turn gold. They were reverting to their changeling forms.

"Dax to Sisko," his communicator said with a chirp. "We just picked up a small Jem'Hadar ship on our scanners. It was hiding on a Bajoran moon. Now it's heading for the wormhole at high speed. Do you want the *Defiant* to give chase?"

Sisko tapped his badge, frowning. "No, Dax," he said. "it's too late. We can't possibly catch them." *And what would we do with them once we caught them?* he wondered.

"But at least another changeling plot has been stopped," Bashir said. "That's the important thing."

"Thanks to *me,*" Vedek Werron said, puffing out his chest.

Sisko shot a glare at him, and the Vedek shut up suddenly. They both knew he'd only accused Mekkar as an excuse to harass the Cardassians. Now leave it to the Vedek to claim he'd seen the whole thing— probably in a vision based on one of the ancient Bajoran prophecies, Sisko thought.

All the other ambassadors were staring at him in shock. Even DuQuesne and Mekkar had run out of insults for once.

"What happened with your DNA scanner?" Sisko asked Bashir. He'd watched the Valtusians pass the test on the docking ring. How had they fooled the computer?

Bashir hesitated. "They must have had real Valtusians aboard their ship," he said. "When they left us to confer—"

"They must have gone inside and taken skin samples," Sisko finished. He nodded; it all made sense now. Like his father had said, they would find a way around any security measures the Federation came up with. It had only taken them ten minutes. So much for any technological advantage a DNA scanner might give them.

"Skin samples . . . or worse." Bashir swallowed visibly, and Sisko realized he must be thinking of severed limbs. "I'd better get over to their ship. I think it's still docked." Turning, he sprinted for the door, calling for medical backup to meet him there. Sisko knew he'd get a full report later. Hopefully there weren't injured or maimed Valtusians being held prisoner aboard the changelings' ship.

Now, though, he had the ruins of the peace conference to deal with. Admiral Dulev would definitely *not* be pleased, he thought.

"I'm sorry," DuQuesne said to him, sounding sincerely apologetic. "It seems we were on the verge of giving the changelings exactly what they wanted."

"The Maquis buffer state might have given the changelings a toehold in the Alpha Quadrant," T'Pao mused. "They might have taken over and used it as a base to launch their invasion of the rest of the Alpha Quadrant."

"It's possible," Sisko said.

Gul Mekkar looked at the other negotiators. "I move for an adjournment for today," he said. "We can reconvene tomorrow to finish up. Not," he added hastily, "that we can use the Valtusian—rather, the *changeling*—plan now, of course. But we can officially dismiss their plan. And perhaps something new will occur to us."

Sisko nodded. "I think that's wise." Although nothing was likely to come of these talks now, the negotiators could still wrap things up nicely. At least they hadn't made a terrible mistake.

Mekkar rose, picking up his files, and nodded to the other Cardassian negotiators. They joined him, heading for the door.

Suddenly an explosion rocked the station. As the floor bucked and heaved beneath him, Sisko rolled with it as best he could, ignoring the panicked screams and shouts from the ambassadors. Alarms began to blare.

"Keep calm!" he shouted over the noise. "Hold on to something and try to stay where you are!"

Was it an attack? Had the Jem'Hadar ship returned and opened fire on them? If so, why hadn't Dax warned him?

Desperately he gripped the edge of the table to keep his balance, then tapped his badge. Smoke began to fill the room. Then everything went dark as power failed. A second later, red emergency lights flickered to life.

"Dax!" he cried. "Status report!"

A second explosion hit, and the force of it knocked him flying backward. He tried to grab hold of something for support. Smoke and red flames leaped everywhere.

"Dax?" he screamed. *Dax?*

CHAPTER
23

KIRA SWALLOWED HARD, feeling like she'd just walked into a nest of pit spiders. Her every instinct made her want to grab her phaser and duck for cover, but she knew she'd be dead before she made it two steps.

"My name is Kira Nerys," she said. "I'm looking for a Groxxin named Orvor. Has anyone here seen him?"

"What do you want with him?" one of the aliens called from the bar. She couldn't see which one, but she thought the voice came from a green glob with three eyes and five or six bony ridges on its broad face.

"Our business is with him alone," she said. "We're not here to start trouble."

"Dead, you won't," another voice called. There were chuckles all around.

"Let me handle this," Worf said to her in a low voice. "I am a trained security officer, after all."

"By all means," Kira said.

Worf stepped forward. "I speak for my companions and myself," he said. "We offer you no threat. Put down your weapons."

Nobody answered. Kira scanned the hard faces looking at them and thought they were getting ready to open fire. She'd better do something fast, she thought, or they'd all end up little piles of ashes.

"You have five seconds to live," the bartender said. "Any last words?"

Worf frowned and opened his mouth, but before he could speak, Kira stepped forward.

"Just . . . *hyperspace links lead us all together.*"

It was the password phrase they had been given so they'd know the real Orvor when they met him. There didn't seem to be much choice but to use it now. Hopefully the Groxxin was somewhere in the room, and hopefully he'd act to save them. It was a long shot, she knew, but she didn't have a better idea.

Instead of one person stepping forward, everyone in the Empty Coffin seemed to relax a little, almost as though she'd passed some test. Did they all know that password? She felt a wave of confusion.

"What about that one?" the bartender demanded, nodding toward Odo. "Isn't he . . .?"

"A changeling, yes," Kira said.

"I am Odo, not 'that one,'" Odo said. "I was brought up in the Alpha Quadrant, and I have renounced the Founders and their philosophy."

"I've never seen a Founder before," the bartender said, lowering his disruptor rifle, "but we all know enough to fear them and their evil ways."

"They are powerful," Odo said. "Determined, yes. Wrong, yes. And certainly stubborn. But not evil."

"So you're defending them—"

"No, I'm saying they're *wrong.*"

"But . . ."

Quietly, Kira drifted toward the back of the bar, searching for a Groxxin. Most of the patrons had put their disruptors away. Half of them were following the bartender's argument with Odo, but the other half had resumed their own conversations.

Kira spotted an alien with dense yellow fur sitting alone in one of the booths. She slid in opposite him, noting his snoutlike mouth and eight-fingered hands. A Groxxin . . . but was he the one they wanted?

"Orvor?" she asked.

The Groxxin shook his head. "He was picked up by the Jem'Hadar last night."

"Picked up? What do you mean?"

"They took him on the street outside." He jerked his head toward the door. "It had to be something important. The Jem'Hadar never come to Old Town unless they have to." He chuckled. "Snipers killed six of 'em on their way out."

"Where would they take him?"

"Probably one of the interrogation centers."

"We have to get him out."

The Groxxin laughed bitterly. "Nobody escapes from the Jem'Hadar. He's probably dead already."

Then we've come all this way for nothing. Kira shook her head. "I can't accept that," she said. "If there's a chance he's still alive, we have to try. Where would he be?"

"Try their central interrogation center; it's located on Peace Street." Quickly he gave her directions.

"Thank you," Kira said. She slid out of the booth and rejoined Worf and Odo by the door. Odo's argument with the bartender was still going strong.

"Did you find him?" Worf asked in a low voice.

She shook her head. "He's not here. The Jem'Hadar picked him up."

"It's not their *nature* to be evil," she heard Odo saying a trifle hotly, "just as there is no species or race that is evil. It's a matter of environment and circumstances. I personally am proof of that, as you can see—"

"I hate to break up this fascinating argument," Kira said, taking Odo by the arm, "but we have to go." She pulled him out the door and onto the street, turned left, and began to walk at a brisk pace. Quickly she told them what the Groxxin had said about Orvor being captured by the Jem'Hadar.

Odo stopped suddenly, looking pained. "I must be the reason," he said.

Kira and Worf stopped, too. "What do you mean?" Worf demanded.

"I mingled with one of the changelings. Just as I felt Selann's thoughts, he must have felt mine as well. He could easily have discovered you were on the

Jem'Hadar ship and learned about Orvor from me. I feel like a fool," he added bitterly.

"That's all right, Odo," Kira said quickly. She knew he would never had consciously given them away. "You couldn't help it. It's not your fault. We wouldn't have made it this far without you. Besides, maybe it's a coincidence. The Jem'Hadar never tried to find us aboard their ship, after all."

"Perhaps," Worf suggested, glowering a bit at Odo, "that's what the hunt was supposed to do. Only we escaped before the net could close in on us."

Kira nodded slowly. Of course, the hunt. She'd been assuming it was aimed at Snoct. Perhaps they had been lucky to get off the Jem'Hadar ship after all.

"But that still leaves our informant," she said, starting forward again. "The Groxxin in the bar seemed to think he would be dead. If so, that's the end of our mission."

"He might still be alive," Odo said. "He would make good bait if they wanted to capture us."

"That's what I was thinking," Worf said. "It smells like a trap."

"I know," Kira said. "But I don't see any alternative other than trying to rescue him. Without him, our whole mission is a waste." *And,* she mentally added, *he and his mate risked their lives to contact us. The least we can do is try.*

The streets had been growing steadily nicer as they walked. Fifteen minutes from Old Town and the Empty Coffin, the first few pedestrians appeared, busting about on unimaginable errands. Now, turning left at a huge apartment complex, Kira abruptly found herself on a broad street lined with open-air shops. Tall spreading trees with razorlike yellow leaves canopied the pavement, and ample street lamps cast a pleasant golden glow over everything. Hundreds, perhaps thousands of people—some Groxxin, some Jem'Hadar, even a few Iffalians like Snoct—moved among the shops, browsing, haggling with merchants, picking up orders. Farther up, a few hovercars glided down the center of the street on antigrav skids.

"Two more blocks," Kira said, eyes searching the buildings ahead. Finally she spotted their target, eight stories tall and built like a prison. "It's that tall stone building—see it?"

"Yes," Worf said.

"There's an alley just ahead," Odo said. "Turn in there."

"Right." Kira ducked into the narrow passageway between two shops selling exotic-looking fruits and vegetables. It was little more than a deep doorway, she realized quickly. They had no real cover here.

There, Odo shapeshifted into a smaller figure with a cloak and a hood that left his face in shadow. He gazed out at Kira.

"Shop close by the building," he said. "I'll go in alone first to make sure it's safe."

"But—"

He shook his head. "I'll be all right, Major," he said. "Nothing can happen to me. You just take care of yourselves for now."

"We'll keep you covered," she promised.

"Keep your weapons hidden," he said. "The last thing I want is to be caught in the middle of a firefight."

He strolled quickly out of the deep doorway, turned, and headed for the interrogation center. Kira watched with trepidation. She had a bad feeling about this whole setup. Now that the changelings knew their plan, what else might they have guessed? *Perhaps Auron hasn't made it back to civilization yet,* she thought, remembering how far they'd stranded him from the Jem'Hadar base on Skovar VI.

She paused at a fruit stand and picked up what looked like a bright purple melon of some kind. When she shook it, it rattled faintly . . . a dried gourd with seeds inside? She passed it to Worf, who smelled it, made a face, and passed it back. Not to his taste either, she thought. She put it back on the stand.

From the corner of her eye, she watched Odo reach the interrogation center. As he climbed the broad steps to the front doors, Jem'Hadar suddenly stormed in from all directions, surrounding Odo with drawn weapons.

CHAPTER
24

MEKKAR DOVE FOR the floor when the first explosion rocked the conference room. It was those damn Bajoran terrorists, he knew. He'd been warned about them by half of his friends before he left Cardassia. *Never turn your back on a Bajoran,* they'd said. *You'll find a dagger in it if you do.*

Close by, someone screamed in agony, and alarm klaxons began to sound. A surge of anger ran through him. Sisko hadn't heard the last of this, he thought.

Smoke roiled around him, thick and choking. Holding his breath, he rose to his knees and peered to the left, trying to spot Kloran or Etkar or any of DS9's security guards. If he only had a disruptor, he thought, they'd stand a chance of making it out of here alive.

His eyes began to sting, and suddenly everything

turned blurry. *It's the smoke.* He blinked at his tears and felt his lungs start to burn. Dropping down as close to the floor as he could, he sucked in a breath of foul-tasting air. At least there didn't seem to be any fire, but that was small consolation.

He began to crawl toward the door, and suddenly he found heavy boots blocking his way. He glanced up and found a phaser pointed at his head. Behind the phaser, wreathed in swirls of smoke, stood a Bajoran with a respirator over his mouth and nose. Hard, angry, fanatically crazy eyes glared down at him.

"Butcher!" the Bajoran cried. He pulled back his leg and kicked with all his strength.

Hardly able to breathe, hardly able to see it coming, Mekkar couldn't dodge in time. The kick caught him in the side of the head, stunning him for a second. He fell, gasping. The Bajoran kicked him a second time, in the side, and he felt ribs crack. Sharp, raw pain blossomed in his side.

Whimpering, he doubled up. What had he done to deserve *this*? he thought. Why did they keep calling him "Butcher"?

"Up!" the Bajoran called, nudging him with the toe of his boot. "On your feet, Mekkar! *Up!*"

Mekkar tried to rise but couldn't get his legs under him. Pain stabbed through his stomach and ribs. He couldn't hold his breath anymore. He sucked in a lungful of smoke and began to cough and wheeze.

Two more Bajorans in respirators joined the first. They seized Mekkar's arms and hauled him forward, through the smoke, to a hole in the wall. They'd blown it open with a bomb of some kind, Mekkar realized. They really *were* insane. They could have depressurized the entire station and killed everyone aboard!

At least the air on the other side tasted better, he thought, wheezing and gasping. If he could just get his breath, maybe he could try to grab a phaser from one of them.

Suddenly someone grabbed his hair and forced his head back. Mekkar found himself staring up at Vedek Werron's hard, cold face.

"Justice," the Vedek said, "will be served."

Turning, the Vedek strode to the door, then out into the corridor. The alarm klaxons were still ringing. People were screaming and running everywhere. Mekkar thought he was going to vomit.

The three Bajorans dragged him down one of the small crossover bridges to the station's core, then up to the Promenade. There, men and women clustered along the huge viewports, trying to see what was going on. The alarms sounded far-off here. Probably more than a few blast doors had already closed, Mekkar thought.

"Help!" he tried to shout. "Help!" What came out was a wracking cough that shook his whole body. They would pay for this, he vowed, as soon as he had his strength back.

Vedek Werron strode into a huge bar like he owned the place. He now had a phaser in each hand, and he fired them both at the ceiling. Mekkar winced, certain they were all going to die from explosive decompression, but the phasers must have been set on stun since nothing happened but bright lights and a whining sound.

Inside, the effect was devastating: Men and woman shrieked and dove for cover.

"Everyone out!" Mekkar ordered. "This place is closed!"

"You can't do that!" a Ferengi called from behind the long bar against the wall.

In answer, Vedek Werron fired both phasers at him.

"Don't shoot! You can do it! You can do it!" the Ferengi called.

Men and women stampeded for the exits, shouting and jostling one another in their haste. As the bar cleared out, the two Bajorans holding Mekkar's arms dragged him to a round table, threw him on top of it, and began tying him spread-eagle across it.

For a second he struggled, but the one on the right turned and punched him in the head as hard as he could. Darkness swept over him.

Quark motioned for Rom to stay down, then peeked around the end of the bar. Two of the Bajorans were tying down their prisoner. Another had taken up a position by the front door. Vedek Werron seated himself at a nearby table, putting both phasers before him. From a pocket he drew a white candle, which he lit and set down before him. He stared at the flame as though in a trance.

They were out of their minds, Quark thought. Did they think they could possibly get away with kidnapping a Cardassian and holing up here? As soon as security arrived, it would be all over. He eased back out of sight.

"What are they doing, brother?" Rom asked in a whisper. Quark didn't think he'd ever seen Rom looking so frightened. Nothing like a true emergency to bring out the coward in someone, he thought.

"Not much," Quark said. He was concerned himself, but most important, he wondered how he could possibly turn things to his own advantage. After all, as the Ninth Rule of Acquisition said, "Opportunity plus instinct equals profit." And his every instinct said he was looking at a latinum-plated opportunity.

Sisko watched as Dax used the station's internal sensors to locate Mekkar. "He's in Quark's," she said.

"Quark's!" Sisko said. He frowned. If Mekkar had run out for a drink instead of being kidnapped . . .

"I'm picking up seven life-forms there," Dax went on. "One Cardassian, four Bajorans, and two Ferengi. Wait—I lost them!" She looked up. "They've activated a scrambler of some kind."

Sisko moved to the transporter controls. Maybe that one brief lock had been enough, he thought. He fed the readings from Dax's console to the transporter and tried to get a lock on Mekkar.

Nothing. "I can't beam Mekkar out," Sisko asked.

"It's a subspace distortion field," Dax went on. "I might be able to punch through it in time, but I couldn't guarantee getting a lock on any of them."

Sisko nodded slowly. "I see." They also might kill

Mekkar at the first sign of trouble, he thought. "I guess we'll have to see what their demands are."

He opened a comm link to Quark's, and a second later Quark's face appeared on the screen.

"Captain Sisko!" Quark said, looking anxious. "I insist you do something at once! There are Bajoran terrorists here—"

A fist flashed in front of the monitor, and Quark gave a pained cry. Everything blurred, and then the monitor swiveled around and Sisko found himself gazing at Vedek Werron's face. Werron smiled serenely.

"Captain Sisko," he said, "the Bajoran people have spoken. War crimes must be atoned for."

Sisko leaned forward, the muscles in his jaw clenching. He had seldom been this angry. It nearly left him speechless.

"Werron," he said, deliberately keeping his words short and clipped. "Put down your weapons, bring Gul Mekkar out, and I promise you that we will get to the bottom of this matter."

"You had your chance, Captain," Werron said. "Here are my demands. You will make a runabout available to me immediately. We will transport the Butcher down to Bajor for a fair trial. After his execution, your peace negotiations can continue."

"And the alternative?" Sisko asked.

"I will convene a military trial here, with myself as judge, jury, and executioner," he said.

"That is unacceptable," Sisko said. Either way, he knew Mekkar would be killed.

"It's your only choice. Think about it." Werron severed the transmission.

"But I've never even been to Bajor before!" Gul Mekkar continued to protest. "This is insane! I was busy fighting the Federation during the Bajoran occupation—"

"Lies!" Werron hissed. His face twisted with rage. "Shut up, Butcher, or I'll kill you here myself!"

Mekkar shut up. Pain speared his side from the broken ribs again, and he twisted in agony on the table. Somehow, he managed to keep from screaming. He wouldn't give Werron the satisfaction.

Quark nursed his bruised cheek. He thought Vedek Werron had loosened a tooth, and he probed carefully with his tongue, tasting blood. So much for reasoning with him, he thought, glaring from across the room.

"Are you all right, brother?" Rom whispered.

"Yes," Quark said, "so far."

"Do yourself a favor . . . leave them alone! It's none of our business what they do to the Cardassian!"

"You're right," Quark said. "It's none of our business. But I'm not going to let him treat me this way in my own bar!"

He slid off his stool and stalked forward. Rom grabbed his arm, pleading silently with him for reason, but Quark shrugged him away.

"Vedek," he said, "there's no reason to let our misunderstanding get in the way of business. Would you like to run a tab while you're staying here?"

Werron stared coldly at him. "So you can poison me?" he demanded.

That was the general idea, Quark thought. "No, of course not!" he said magnanimously. "Corpses are bad for business. I'm just trying to make an honest living, that's all."

"Water," Werron said.

"That's it?" Quark asked. "Would you like it scented, perhaps? Or flavored with Jonja? Or perhaps—"

"Water," Werron said. "Pure, unadulterated water."

"Coming up," Quark said. Turning, he headed for the bar. He could feel Werron's sharp gaze boring into the back of his head, and he shivered a little. No chance of drugging the Vedek's water, he thought, but if he could win his trust, maybe he'd try some Bajoran spiced ale later. You could hide some pretty potent solutions in that, and he'd never know until it hit him. . . .

Sisko bit his lip and considered the problem from every angle. It seemed to come down to two choices, neither of which appealed to him: Let Werron and his people kill Mekkar on the station or let them transport Mekkar down to Bajor for trial and execution. He had no doubt that an armed attack on Quark's bar would result in Mekkar's immediate execution, and it might also cost the lives of some of the Bajorans and his own security forces. This would have been a perfect job for Odo, he reflected.

He'd scarcely had time to think about the mission to the Gamma Quadrant, he realized a bit guiltily. Too much had been going on here. He prayed they were having better luck than he was.

Now he had to focus on the present problem, however. What options did he have?

What if I let them take Mekkar to Bajor? he wondered. *That would at least buy us more time. And if he's guilty of war crimes, perhaps he should be punished . . . but through the proper channels.*

He realized suddenly that he didn't know whether Mekkar really was this so-called Butcher of Belmast, as all the Bajorans seemed to believe. Dax hadn't had time to give him her full report.

"What about Mekkar?" he asked her. *"Is* he guilty of war crimes?"

"No," she said. "Gul *Rel* Mekkar—our Mekkar—is innocent. He had never even been in Bajoran space before these peace negotiations, which is why the Detepa Council sent him. They had hoped to avoid any problems with the Bajorans. According to Bajoran records I was able to access, Gul *Ren* Mekkar—similar name, similar appearance, perhaps a relative of our Mekkar—was the one the Bajorans called the Butcher of Belmast."

"It seems a pretty clear case of mistaken identity," he said. "How could Werron have made such a mistake?"

"He *wants* to believe Mekkar is the Butcher of Belmast," Dax said. "Everything I've read about him leads me to believe he's not stable. He thinks he has a divine responsibility to bring all Cardassians to justice. This hostage taking . . ." She shook her head. "He's a dangerous man, and nothing's going to convince him he's wrong. Not even the facts."

"I have to try," Sisko said.

He called Quark's bar again, and this time Werron answered himself.

"I've had a chance to review the facts of the Belmast case," Sisko said, "and I agree that it's an outrage, and appropriate steps should be taken to punish the guilty parties."

"Excellent," Werron said. "Then you'll provide a transport for us to Bajor."

"I said the *guilty* parties, Vedek. Gul Rel Mekkar isn't the Butcher of Belmast. He's never even been to Bajor. You're looking for Gul *Ren* Mekkar—"

"Lies!" Werron screamed. "All lies!"

Slowly Sisko shook his head. "Facts don't lie, Vedek. If you don't believe me, I'll be glad to supply you with the appropriate files so you can check for yourself—"

"Get me that runabout," Mekkar said. His eyes were wild, dangerous, Sisko thought. "You have one hour."

He severed the connection.

"He's a fanatic," Dax said. "There's no reasoning with him."

Sisko sighed. "I'm starting to think you're right," he said. "I'll have to seek a higher authority."

"Admiral Dulev?"

"Kai Winn," he said. As the religious leader of

Bajor, she might have enough influence with Werron to talk sense into him, he thought. "Try to keep an eye on Werron," he said. "Let me know if anything happens."

"You got it," she said.

Sisko went into his office and shut the door. He didn't particularly like Kai Winn, but he understood her. Although she had a ruthless—and sometimes senseless—drive for power, hers was an honest greed compared to Werron's.

He put through the call. Would she speak to him? Would she be available on such short notice? After a few tense moments of waiting, her face appeared on the monitor.

"Hello, Emissary," she said, smiling broadly. She did beatific well, he thought. "As always, it is a pleasure to speak with you."

"And it's a pleasure to see you looking so well," he said. "I have a problem with Vedek Werron, however, and I was hoping you might be able to give me the benefit of your counsel."

She all but preened herself in satisfaction. Nothing worked quite so well as playing up to her, he thought.

Quickly he outlined the situation. "Vedek Werron seems unwilling to listen to reason—or the truth."

Kai Winn sighed. "Werron has always been something of a problem for us," she said. "If Mekkar is not the Butcher, he should be released at once. We don't want another Cardassian incident; this is an age of healing. We must move on and put the scars of the past behind us."

"Exactly," Sisko said. "Then you'll speak to him for us."

"He would never listen to me," she said. "He has somehow built me up in his mind as his enemy. He thinks he sees plots of my spinning behind every bush and every tree."

"Then what do you suggest?"

"Send him to Bajor. We will have a fair trial for Gul Mekkar, and I will personally expedite it. We will have him declared innocent and released, if that is the case, within a single day."

Sisko smiled. "Thank you, Kai," he said. That sounded like an altogether satisfactory solution.

CHAPTER 25

THE SECOND THE Jem'Hadar surrounded him, Odo let his body loose its rigid form, morphing back into his normal humanoid shape. The change served no real purpose except to show them that he *could* shapeshift—that he was, in fact, a changeling. Hopefully that would be enough.

"Founder," the leader of the Jem'Hadar squad said, dropping to his knees.

Odo turned slowly. Every one of his attackers had bowed down before him, he saw. They were no different than the other Jem'Hadar he'd encountered. They had been genetically programmed to feel awe, respect, and dedication bordering on devotion to any changeling they encountered. Well, he thought, if they wanted a Founder, he'd play the part.

"What is the meaning of this attack?" he demanded, trying to sound as irritated as possible. Now that he thought back to their joining, he remembered Selann's memories of dealing with Jem'Hadar. The changeling always used this same tone.

"Sir," the leader said, meeting his gaze. "This is a trap to find and capture the Federation spies—"

"Enough," Odo said, waving one hand curtly. "Send your men back to their positions. If your real targets show up, I trust you'll do a better job of capturing them."

"Yes, Founder." He saluted, then rose and sent his men back to their hiding places.

Odo watched expressionlessly as the Jem'Hadar fitted themselves into the shadows, behind market stands, and down in recessed doorways. If he hadn't known they were there, he never would have spotted them, he realized. Only the officer remained out of position, next to him.

The trap also confirmed his worst fears, Odo thought: Selann had indeed picked up on the details of their mission while they had been joined. He'd have to watch out for that in the future, he knew.

Turning, he strolled up the steps toward the interrogation center's front doors. He felt a flash of apprehension as the officer kept pace with him.

"Is there anything I can do for you?" the officer asked.

"I am here to interrogate the prisoner," Odo said.

"Which one?"

Which one? There's more than one? He'd better

bluff, he thought. No—he had a better idea. What would Selann have done in this situation?

He whirled and glared down at the Jem'Hadar. "You forget your place, Soldier. When you need information, you will be provided with it."

The officer's face fell. Odo strode forward alone. It had worked, he thought triumphantly.

The huge door slid aside for him, and he found himself in a long, high chamber. The walls and floor, made of some amber-colored stone, had been polished to mirror smoothness. Except for a single guard fifty meters ahead, the place seemed deserted.

His footsteps echoed loudly as he moved forward. The guard snapped to attention, staring at Odo.

"Where are prisoners held?" Odo demanded as he neared.

"Level three, Founder," the guard said without hesitation.

Odo gave a nod, then stepped up to one of the turbolifts. The doors slid open for him. He entered without a backward glance. Let them think he knew what he was doing, he thought.

"Level three," he said.

Instead of heading up, though, the lift headed down. When the doors opened again, this time onto a narrow corridor, two more Jem'Hadar guards snapped to attention. Odo strode past them without so much as acknowledging their existence. *Selann should see me now,* he thought. The changeling had inadvertently provided him with better training to infiltrate this Jem'Hadar prison than he would ever have expected.

The corridor opened onto the interrogation center's holding area. It was odd, Odo noted, how uniform prisons seemed to be across the galaxy. They fell into two categories. If you came from a high technology, you used force fields. If you came from a low technology, you used metal bars.

This prison was of the low-tech variety. Each cell had been cut into solid bedrock. Durasteel bars ran from the floor to the ceiling along the front wall. There had to be hundreds of cells on this level, he thought, moving forward between rows of cells. Some prisoners stared sullenly out at him. Others lay with their faces turned to the stone wall. Several wept openly. Odo felt a wave of sympathy and wished he could do more. Although the cells looked clean enough, there was an atmosphere of doom about the place. No wonder the Groxxin in the Empty Coffin had said nobody ever escaped from the interrogation center.

Finally he came to a cell with a yellow-furred Groxxin inside. He lay on his bench staring up into infinity with large round eyes. Manacles held his wrists to the wall. Half-healed burn wounds covered his arms. Odo felt a rush of anger at seeing a prisoner treated in such a manner. He couldn't stand the idea of torture—he found the concept criminal.

"You are Orvor?" he said, trying to sound authoritative.

"What of it?" The Groxxin sneered openly at him.

The prisoner's spirit hadn't been broken yet, Odo saw. That had to be a good sign. Perhaps he hadn't talked yet. He still might have the retrovirus that would unlock the Jem'Hadar's DNA.

Odo risked a sidelong glance up the corridor. The two guards hadn't moved. They were muttering quietly between each other and watching him, though. What would be the best way to handle the situation? What would a real Founder do if he wanted to remove a prisoner?

"You," he called loudly to one of the guards. "Come here."

The Jem'Hadar hurried over. "Yes, Founder," he said.

"Who is this one?" Odo demanded.

"A Groxxin terrorist."

"Has he talked yet?"

"Not yet, Founder."

"What are you doing about that?"

"Standard procedure. He will be interrogated again tomorrow, and if he still proves uncooperative, he will be terminated."

Odo nodded. He didn't have much time left. "I wish to interrogate this one myself," he said.

"Sir?"

Odo whirled and struck him across the face. "Do not question me! *Move!*"

"Yes, Founder."

Quickly the guard unlocked the cell door, stepped

in, and released Orvor's manacles from their magnetic clamps to the wall. Orvor rose with a sigh and shuffled out, his chains rattling.

"I won't talk," he said.

"We'll see about that," Odo countered. He looked at the Jem'Hadar. "The keys to his restraints?"

Silently the guard passed them over. Then, pulling Orvor along by his manacles, Odo turned and led him down the corridor and into the turbolift.

The doors closed, and they started up.

"Pause," Odo said to the computer. "Lock access to this turbolift."

"What are you doing?" Orvor demanded.

"Hyperspace links lead us all together," Odo said, unlocking the manacles and pulling them off of Orvor's wrists and ankles.

"But you're—"

"Yes," Odo said. "I don't have time to explain. I'm here with two others to get you out." He pushed the manacles into the corner, where they couldn't be seen from outside the turbolift. It would have to do, he decided.

Standing, he said, "Resume. Surface level."

The lift started upward once more.

When the doors opened, Odo half expected to see changelings and more Jem'Hadar waiting for him, but the one guard still stood there. He snapped to attention again as Odo and Orvor walked past him.

Together, side by side, they walked out the front door and down the steps. Odo felt the eyes of the hidden Jem'Hadar on him, but he didn't acknowledge their presence in any way. He simply walked out to the middle of the street, turned left, and kept going.

He spotted Kira and Worf at one of the fruit stands. They saw him, then followed at a leisurely pace, as though they were casual shoppers moving on to a different stand.

Six blocks from the interrogation center, Odo began to think they might get away with it. Twenty blocks later, as the crowds thinned out, he knew they had. He turned down a side alley and paused, and a few seconds later Kira and Worf joined them.

"This is Orvor," Odo said, and he made the introductions.

"We did it!" Kira grinned and slapped him on the back. Worf nodded solemnly.

"All we have to do is get back to our ship," Odo said.

"Tell me . . . my wife?" Orvor began.

"She's safe," Kira said. "You'll be back with her in three days, maybe sooner if the debriefing goes well."

Orvor shook his head. "There won't be any debriefing," he said.

Odo tensed. "Why?"

"The retrovirus—they took the files when they arrested me. I'm afraid you've come for nothing."

"We'll discuss that later," Odo said. "Right now we've got to get out of here. As soon as they discover you're gone, this place is going to be crawling with Jem'Hadar looking for us."

He nodded. "You're right. Which way to your ship?"

Odo took the lead. Once more they passed through Old Town, and once more he glimpsed furtive figures paralleling them, trying to gauge their strength, trying to work up their courage to attack. Kira and Worf drew their phasers and carried them openly. That seemed to turn the trick, Odo saw. They made it to the spaceport's landing field unscathed.

As soon as they stepped onto the duracrete, into the brightness of the landing field's lights, Odo felt almost safe. They headed up the row of shuttles. He began counting, so he'd know exactly where they'd left their ship.

When they got there, though, he stopped in shock. Their berth between the two Jem'Hadar warships lay empty.

Their ship had vanished.

CHAPTER
26

Sisko took a second runabout to Bajor with Dax and Dr. Bashir aboard, following the ship he'd loaned to Vedek Werron. Sisko kept a careful eye on the sensors. For all he knew, Werron might throw Mekkar out an airlock along the way.

But it seemed Vedek Werron truly did intend to turn Mekkar over to the authorities. The Vedek landed his ship in a field just outside the small southern city of Belmast—the site where Mekkar had supposedly committed his atrocities—and Sisko brought his own runabout down there, too.

Thousands of Bajorans had turned out to meet the runabouts, Sisko saw, and lines of Bajoran security guards held them back a safe distance. Some of the crowd held up placards saluting Werron. Others held signs in various languages screaming for justice and death for the Butcher of Belmast. News reporters swarmed everywhere with cameras.

"It looks like quite a welcoming committee," Dax commented.

"A circus is more like it," Sisko said.

Bashir said, "Let's hope they're friendly."

"I didn't allow Mekkar to be brought here only to have him lynched," Sisko said. Rising, he opened the hatch and hopped to the ground.

The noise was incredible, Sisko thought, staring out at the thousands of Bajorans being held back by a line of security guards. They all seemed to be screaming insults directed at Mekkar. Dax joined him, then Bashir. Dax shouted something to him, but he couldn't make out the words; he tapped to his ears and shook his head. She nodded and pointed to the other runabout.

Sisko turned. The hatch had opened and now Vedek Werron climbed out. He raised both arms in salutation, and the crowd went wild. Sisko had to cover his ears. Next, following him, came two of the Vedek's followers, and they dragged a limp Gul Mekkar between them. Mekkar appeared unconscious—or so Sisko hoped. That was infinitely better than dead.

A few people in the crowd began throwing stones. One struck Mekkar on the cheek, opening a jagged wound. Dark blood flowed out.

Bajoran security officers hurried forward, seized Mekkar's arms, and hustled him to a waiting vehicle.

It looked heavily armored, Sisko saw. The guards locked themselves inside, then the vehicle took off, flying low over the crowd. A few more rocks struck its sides, then it accelerated toward the city and rapidly vanished from sight.

The security officers let down their crowd-control barriers, and the mob surged forward, heading for Werron and his men. They lifted the Vedek into the air and began parading him forward. Grinning, Werron waved to everyone around him.

He's quite the hero now, Sisko thought. But what would the Bajorans think when they found out the truth?

Spontaneously most of the crowd began to sing a battle hymn Sisko had never heard before. Still singing, they bore Werron and his followers off toward the center of the city. Five minutes later, they were alone.

Bashir was shaking his head. "I've never seen anything like that," he said. "It was . . . incredible."

"I think we'd better see the local authorities," Sisko said, "before this thing gets any more out of control." He glanced at Dax. As soon as they'd learned Vedek Werron's destination, she'd looked up the city on the ship's database. "Which way?"

"That tall building with the spires," she said, pointing to the left, "is the Hall of Justice."

Three hours and ten meetings later, Sisko had a bad feeling in his stomach. True to her word, Kai Winn had expedited proceedings. Unfortunately, she'd failed to tell anyone that Mekkar wasn't the Butcher of Belmast. Every official who met with Sisko insisted Mekkar would get a fair trial—"All of Bajor is watching, after all!"—and then went on to say that his execution had been scheduled for the following week.

They weren't taking him seriously, Sisko realized. They all *wanted* Mekkar to be guilty. Like Vedek Werron, they saw what they wanted to see and nothing else.

At one point he saw a photograph of the real Butcher of Belmast. The moment he did, he realized where the mistake had come from. The two Cardassians looked enough alike to be identical twins. *But that doesn't help our Gul Mekkar,* he thought.

Worst of all, Kai Winn suddenly made herself unavailable to talk whenever Sisko called. He began to grow frustrated. He started to think he'd been duped by her. She hadn't believed him and had used him to bring Mekkar to Bajor for trial. Gul Mekkar really *was* going to be tried and, Sisko assumed, found guilty and executed for crimes he did not commit.

"Nobody here will speak on the Butcher's behalf," a frustrated magistrate finally snapped at Sisko after a long argument about due process. "Since you think the Butcher's innocent, why don't you have yourself appointed as his Speaker?"

Dax leaned close and whispered, "That might not be a bad idea, Benjamin. As I understand the judicial system in Belmast, it will give you a lot more leeway to present Mekkar's case."

That made sense. "Is there a downside?" he asked her.

"If you plead his case and lose, it's bound to affect your standing as the Emissary."

"That's a chance I'm willing to take." Sisko nodded to the magistrate. "Very well. What do I need to do to become Mekkar's Speaker?"

"I have the forms . . . Yes! Here we are." He handed Sisko a set of pages.

Sisko signed everywhere he indicated. "That's it?" he asked as he finished.

"Yes," the magistrate said. "The trial begins at first light tomorrow. Be here an hour beforehand to see the Butcher."

"I want to see him now."

"Impossible."

Sisko barely managed to keep his anger in check. This wasn't a trial, it was murder. He'd never run into so many roadblocks before. They didn't want justice, he realized, they wanted blood. *Mekkar's* blood.

Dax took his arm and pulled him from the magistrate's office. "I know that look," she said. "You were going to do something you'd regret."

He sighed. "You're probably right. What do you suggest?"

"Let's find Julian and get back to the runabout. We're going to have a lot of work to do to get ready for that trial tomorrow."

He tapped his badge. "Sisko to Bashir. Where are you, Doctor?"

"I've just been to see Gul Mekkar," Bashir replied.

"What? How?" Sisko could barely believe it. They hadn't let him anywhere near Mekkar's cell.

"I explained that he was hurt and I was his personal physician. They want him in top health for his execution, it seems."

"How is he?"

"Two broken ribs, some cuts and bruises, a slight case of shock. I've done as much for him as I could, all things considered. I'd really like to get him back to DS9. How are you coming?"

"Not well," Sisko said. "The trial begins tomorrow."

Sisko spent the rest of the night cramming through Bajoran legal precedents. Bleary-eyed, he finally allowed Dr. Bashir to give him a light stimulant to keep him awake. Mekkar's life was in danger; he knew he had to be sharp for the trial. The Bajorans seemed to think it wouldn't last more than one or possibly two days at the most. He had no intention of letting them railroad Mekkar into a punishment he didn't deserve.

Dax and Bashir pursued other lines of inquiry. Dax was trying to get information on the real Butcher of Belmast from Cardassia, but kept running into roadblocks. Bashir was looking for medical reasons to postpone the trial. Neither made fast progress.

The night passed all too quickly. Finally it was nearly time to head to the Hall of Justice. Sisko sighed and tabbed off the computer monitor, rubbing his eyes. What he really needed, he thought, was a team of crack Federation legal experts, six months to prepare for the trial, and some Bajoran advisors to help him over the rough spots. Nevertheless, he would have to make do and trust in the truth to win out.

After cleaning himself up as best he could in the runabout, he headed for the courtroom, Dax at his side. Bashir was still at work.

"I'll catch up," he promised, "as soon as I have something."

"It had better be fast," Sisko said. "I have a feeling this is going to be a very quick trial, if we're not careful."

"Right." Swallowing, Bashir threw himself back into his work.

It was a twenty-minute walk to the center of Belmast. By the time Sisko and Dax arrived, a huge crowd had already gathered outside. He had to push his way through. It seemed most of the city had turned out to wait for the guilty verdict, Sisko thought. It was a shame he had to disappoint them.

Inside, a guard ushered them into a huge, cavernous room where the trial would take place. Security seemed tight. At the far end of the room, on a raised dais, sat the three magistrates who would hear the case. One of them, he saw, was the Bajoran who'd suggested he act as Mekkar's Speaker. For a second he considered asking the man to remove himself from the case—after all, he'd already made up his mind that Mekkar was guilty, but then Sisko thought better of it. All three magistrates undoubtedly felt the same way. Trying to remove one might aggravate matters. No, he would have to win them over.

"Over here," the guard said, leading them to one side. A table had been set up for them.

"Thank you," Sisko said. He glanced to the right, where another table sat: probably for the prosecution. The two Bajorans there ignored him.

The magistrates signaled their readiness. Mekkar, in chains but walking—no doubt thanks to Bashir, Sisko thought—was escorted in. He sat in the center of the hall, facing the three magistrates. Sisko sat behind Mekkar and to the left; the Prosecutor sat to the right.

The magistrate in the center rose. "This trial is open," he said loudly, and his voice echoed through the vast Hall of Justice. "Read the charges."

The Prosecutor rose. "Gul Mekkar, known as the Butcher of Belmast, is accused of the following crimes against Bajor. First, that he did knowingly and willfully order the death of two thousand three hundred and twelve mine-workers following the Ten Day Strike. Second, that he did knowingly and willfully order the executions of four hundred and sixty-five Bajorans following a food riot in Belmast. Third—"

The list of crimes went on and on. Sisko listened, and as he did his horror grew. The real Mekkar had been a bloodthirsty monster, he realized, drunk on power. No wonder everyone on Bajor wanted him brought to justice.

Nearly two hours later, the Prosecutor finished his list of crimes.

"How say you to these charges?" the magistrate asked.

Sisko rose slowly. When he turned, it was to address not only the magistrates, but the Prosecutor and all the Bajorans who had assembled inside the Hall of Justice.

"I am Captain Benjamin Sisko," he said, "the commanding officer of *Deep Space Nine*. You all know who I am, and believe me, no one has more sympathy for the Bajoran people than I do. Kai Opara proclaimed me your Emissary, and I have walked in the wormhole with the beings you call Prophets.

"You all suffered tremendously under the Cardassian occupation. But this is now a time for healing and reconciliation. Cardassians are not your enemies. They are a people like any other—some good, some bad."

"Is there a point to this?" the Prosecutor asked dryly.

"Yes." Sisko took a deep breath and scanned the faces around him. "Mekkar is an innocent man. He was not here during the Cardassian occupation. True, there is a similarity in names, and true, there is a similarity in appearance. He is a distant relative of the so-called Butcher of Belmast. You cannot convict him for crimes he did not commit!"

"You have evidence of this, of course," said the magistrate on the left.

"Yes. If I may present it?"

"Proceed."

"My science officer, Lieutenant Commander Dax,

has gathered the following information from the Cardassian government." Sisko nodded to Dax.

Dax picked up a set of folders from the Speaker's table and carried them forward. She handed one to each of the magistrates, one to the Prosecutor, and one to Sisko.

"Thank you, Dax," he said.

She smiled and returned to her seat.

Sisko opened the folder. The first page held two pictures side by side, one of the real Gul Mekkar as he had been during the occupation—and the similarity to their Mekkar *was* striking—and one as the real Gul Mekkar was today.

"Here you see these two different Cardassians," he began.

"I see no difference," the Prosecutor said. "These photos are of the same person."

"They are different—" Sisko began.

The magistrate cut him off. "What proof do you have?" he asked. "Photos and documents can be faked."

"Proof?" Sisko said. He'd been afraid they would say something like that. Dax had been trying to get through to Cardassia to get direct confirmation all night without success. At the moment, they had only his word, which might not be enough. "Look at the pictures. They have Starfleet authentication. You have my word as the Emissary and as a Starfleet officer. *Mekkar is not guilty of these crimes.*"

The three magistrates conferred briefly. Sisko watched anxiously as they compared the two photographs, studied the two Mekkars' identifications, life histories, and war records. They frowned, then nodded.

Sisko's badge chirped. He tapped it as subtly as he could. "Yes?" he whispered.

"It's Bashir," he heard the doctor say. "I've finally reached Cardassia—"

"Hold that thought, Doctor," he said.

An undercurrent of talking had swept through the Hall of Justice while the magistrates studied Sisko's evidence. The magistrate in the middle looked up suddenly.

"Silence!" he roared.

"This evidence is not conclusive," the magistrate to his left said. "We took nearly three hundred sworn testimonies yesterday identifying this Cardassian as the Butcher of Belmast. Since you are unable to produce concrete evidence—"

"Wait!" Sisko cried. "Did you hear that, Doctor?" he said. "Do you have someone on line now who can clear our Mekkar?"

"I think so," Bashir said. "Is there a monitor there? I can relay the signal through."

Sisko looked up at the magistrates, who gave a brief nod.

"Do so," Sisko said. He swallowed. Whatever Bashir had found, it had better be good, he thought.

A clerk activated a holographic projector, and a huge image flickered to life on one side of the Hall of Justice. It was Bashir.

"This image is being sent to us directly from

Cardassia PMMR," Bashir said. "It's not the highest quality signal, considering the distances involved. But I think it will do."

He touched a button before them.

Static flickered on the screen, and then an older Cardassian appeared. He looked like Gul Mekkar, only a long thin scar puckered the left side of his mouth.

"I am," the Cardassian said in a low, powerful voice, "Gul Ren Mekkar, whom Bajoran terrorists branded the Butcher of Belmast nearly twenty years ago." He scanned the faces of the magistrates, and a faint sneer crept into his voice. "Bajorans are a little people," he said, "hardly worth the attention of a proud and great race like the Cardassians. I spat on you then, and I spit on you now."

The magistrate on the right stood. "You—" he said, voice hoarse. "You killed my father and my grandfather."

Mekkar sneered, "And I'd kill you too, given half the chance. If it were up to me, I'd put Bajor back under Cardassian rule tomorrow. We should never have left before we broke your spirits. You—"

"I think that's quite enough," Bashir said, interrupting the tirade. He gazed at the magistrates from the viewscreen. "Or do you want to hear more from him?"

"No . . . no," said the magistrate, sitting. His face was ashen, Sisko saw. He now realized what a mistake they had almost made.

"I want all charges against Gul Mekkar dropped," Sisko said loudly. "He is innocent."

The three magistrates conferred for a minute, then nodded. "Agreed," the high magistrate said. "Release the prisoner," he told the clerk.

Sisko and Dax hurried forward to help Mekkar stand as the clerk unlocked the chains on his arms and legs. Mekkar seemed to be in a state of shock, Sisko thought. Little wonder, considering what he'd just been through. Best to get him back to Bashir and DS9 as quickly as possible.

He put one of Mekkar's arms around his shoulders and Dax did the same. Together, they helped the Cardassian down the long aisle, past the benches filled with silent Bajorans, and outside.

"Thank you," Sisko heard Mekkar whispering. "Thank you."

"That's what I'm here for," he said.

Julian Bashir watched them set Gul Mekkar free, then cut off his transmission to the Hall of Justice. So much for that, he thought. His plan had worked perfectly.

He flipped back to the signal from DS9. It was completely secure, he knew, coming in on a scrambled channel. He found the face of the Butcher of Belmast grinning at him.

"How did I do?" Garak asked behind his makeup.

"Fine," Bashir said. "I think you just saved the day. See you when we get back. I owe you a drink."

"You owe me more than that," Garak said. "I have an Oslan silk suit here with your name on it, Doctor."

Bashir groaned a bit, but didn't complain. It was worth it.

He severed the connection and smiled. There was a certain irony in the solution, he thought. The Bajorans refused to believe the truth, no matter how it had been presented to them. But they'd been only too eager to believe a lie.

CHAPTER
27

"WHERE IS IT?" Kira demanded. A ship didn't just vanish. Someone had moved it . . . or taken it back, she realized with growing panic.

She glanced around. None of the other shuttles seemed to be in use, but she didn't think they'd have sufficient range to make it back to DS9. But they might give the others a place to hide while she looked around.

Then she remembered Snoct Sneyd. He said he'd help them if they ever needed it. Well, she thought, they certainly needed it now.

"Get them over to one of the shuttles and keep them there," she said to Worf. "I'm going to see if I can find Snoct. Maybe he can help us find a new ship."

Worf nodded. "Agreed." He turned to Odo and

Orvor. "This way, quickly," he said, striking out for the nearest shuttle.

Kira hesitated. Where would she find an Iffalian maintenance crew? Probably near the center of the field, she decided. That way they could be quickly dispatched to any ship that needed them.

She took her bearings and started walking.

Twenty minutes later, she saw movement ahead: a small car on antigrav skids. It was filled with Jem'Hadar and was headed straight for her. Turning to the side like she had business at one particular ship, she ducked out of sight.

"You'd better work again," she murmured, activating her cloaker. Instantly the air around her shimmered, and then she seemed to be looking out at the world through a thick glass wall. Everything became muted and distant.

The Jem'Hadar turned where she'd turned and passed not two meters from where she stood. They slowed down, peering this way and that, obviously searching for her. Their starship had been deliberately moved, Kira realized, to prevent them from escaping. The changelings knew what they were up to.

Biting her lip, she turned and sprinted up the landing field, trying to put as much distance between herself and the Jem'Hadar as she could. She only had a few minutes left on her cloaker, she reminded herself. She began to count the seconds.

She put a good half kilometer and ten rows of parked ships between herself and the Jem'Hadar.

That ought to be enough for now, she decided, slowing down and ducking behind another ship, this one a small fighter craft of some sort. She shut off the cloaker and crouched there, panting, until she caught her wind.

Then, carefully, she continued to jog forward. If anything came up, she still had a little time left on the cloaker, she thought. She wished she'd brought Worf's as well. She had a strange feeling she'd need all the help she could get.

A large cluster of buildings appeared on the horizon. That had to be the central complex, she decided. The Iffalians had better be there.

Then she saw movement ahead on the landing field—more Jem'Hadar, she realized. She glanced around in panic. She was a good fifty meters from the nearest cover. She'd never make it before being seen.

She activated her cloaker again, hoping they hadn't spotted her yet. Turning, she jogged quickly to the side, cutting across, and just as quickly she stopped short. A pair of Jem'Hadar warriors were patrolling this area on foot, their disruptors held ready. Beyond them lay a couple of low buildings—little more than storage sheds, really. Maybe she could find cover there.

Suddenly colors flickered all around her. The cloaker had begun running low on power, she realized. Its distortion field shimmered brightly for an instant, like a beacon in the darkness, then returned to normal. She checked its readouts. Less than a minute left, she thought with dismay.

"There!" one of Jem'Hadar began to shout, pointing in her direction.

Kira glanced down. The cloaker failed again, and for the second time a sheet of colored light rippled over her body. She stood out like a burning torch, she realized. Suddenly it failed altogether, and she found herself standing completely exposed.

The two Jem'Hadar fired just as she dived to the side, and their energy bolts sizzled past, just missing her. She ducked around the nearest ship, tucked down her head, and sprinted toward the buildings. Maybe she could lose them there, she thought.

She risked a glance back. The two Jem'Hadar sprinted after her, about twenty yards behind. Gradually they began to close the gap. It would be close, Kira thought, but she'd beat them.

She rounded the first low building, spotted a stack of wooden crates, and skidded behind them without a second's hesitation. The two Jem'Hadar pounded past. One of them glanced her way but didn't spot her in the shadows.

For once, her luck was holding, Kira thought. As soon as they passed by, she got up and took a closer look at the shed. The door lay on the other side, she saw, but there were a few high windows for ventilation on this side. It would be a tight fit, but she thought she could get through.

Climbing onto the crates, she opened the window and glanced inside. It seemed to be a storage depot for heavy cleaning equipment of some kind, she thought.

Grunting a little, she pulled herself in, then lowered herself to the floor.

She heard the patrol returning, more slowly this time. She eased back farther into the darkness. A heartbeat later, a face appeared at the ventilation window she'd climbed through. The Jem'Hadar peered this way and that, but didn't spot her. He tried squeezing inside himself, but rapidly gave up. With his muscles, he'd never fit.

Someone outside shouted something, and he pulled back.

Kira drifted forward like a ghost. Standing on tiptoe, she could just see out the window. More Jem'Hadar had appeared, including two of the cars on antigrav skids, and they began to mill about outside, talking among themselves.

Kira sighed and slumped to the floor, her back to the wall.

It looked like it was going to be a long night, she thought.

Forty minutes later, the Jem'Hadar still hadn't left. They kept wandering by in little groups, as if hoping she'd magically reappear. Perhaps they were waiting for daylight to track her, she thought.

Then she spotted a group of Iffalians walking toward the storage sheds on foot. They looked a lot like Snoct Sneyd, she thought, only they wore drab gray uniforms. She hesitated. Was it worth trying to get them to help her?

They opened the doors of the storage shed next to hers and began wheeling out equipment. They were only twenty meters away. But they were in the open, and if that patrol spotted her, she wouldn't have a prayer of escape.

There had to be some way to attract the Iffalians' attention, she finally decided. She looked around the shed, but in the semidarkness nothing stood out among the large hulking machines. She didn't see a single thing she could use to attract their attention.

She felt her own pockets and also came up empty— just her phaser and the personal cloaker.

Well, valuable or not, she needed to use it. Since it wasn't working, she took the cloaker off, opened up its control panel, and started breaking off little pieces of delicate circuitry. She began stacking them on the floor in front of her.

When she had a little pile of them, she slowly pushed open the ventilation window and threw the first piece toward the Iffalians as hard as she could. It fell a little short; they didn't even look up. Taking a deep breath, she threw the second piece. This one traveled a little farther and came to rest a few meters to the left of one of the workers. He didn't look up, either, though.

"What do I have to do," Kira muttered to herself, "hit you in the head?"

She threw the third piece, and this time her aim came closer. It fell short by a few meters, but skittered forward and tapped one of the workers' boots.

He glanced down, saw the piece of rubbish, and

bent to pick it up curiously. Kira didn't wait, but threw two more pieces in quick succession. She didn't want to lose him now that she had his interest.

The other pieces must have caught his eye. He turned and stared toward her shed. *Come on,* she thought, *just a little bit closer . . .*

He didn't take so much as a step in her direction.

"Psst!" Kira said as loudly as she dared. "Psst! Come over here, quick!"

The alien muttered something to his companions, then picked up a broom and dustpan. He pretended to sweep up bits of rubbish and quickly worked his way over to Kira.

"Who are you?" he demanded in a whisper, not looking in her direction.

"A friend," Kira said. "Do you know Snoct Sneyd?"

"The one who was trapped in the Jem'Hadar ship?"

"Yes. Can you get him for me? I need his help."

"Why?"

"Because I'm trapped here, the Jem'Hadar are looking for me, and he said he owed me a favor. I got him off that ship and saved his life, after all."

"That was you?" The Iffalian looked up at her, an expression of awe and wonder on his face.

"Yes," Kira said. "Can you help me?"

"Wait here."

He worked his way back to the others and conversed briefly with them. Kira watched expectantly, but they did nothing to acknowledge her presence.

Instead, they quickly finished unloading their cleaning equipment and rolled it away.

She sat back. Was that a good sign? Had they decided to turn her in, in case there was a reward? She didn't know. If only Snoct Sneyd had been there, she thought, things would have been much simpler.

She gazed out the window again, straining to see both left and right. There was no sign of the patrol. Perhaps she should make a break for it, she thought, and try to steal a ship on her own. If the Jem'Hadar surrounded her shed, she knew she wouldn't have a chance of escaping.

She had just about decided to strike out again on her own when she spotted the maintenance crew returning, this time with a vehicle. The little transport had a square storage compartment mounted over the rear antigrav skids, she saw. And there were more Iffalians this time. And was that Snoct Sneyd . . .? *Yes,* she thought. *It's him.* Relief flooded through her. He'd come to help.

They opened the doors to her shed and backed the transport up. Snoct darted inside.

"Major Kira!" he said.

"Thanks for coming," she said. "They took our ship—"

"I know," he said. "The Founders ordered it. We're cleaning it for them now."

"Can you take me there?"

"Of course!" he said. He crossed to the storage compartment on the transport and opened the cover. "Climb in!"

"First we need to get Worf and the others," she said.

Snoct Sneyd drove the transport back to where she'd left Worf, Odo, and Orvor. Fortunately, the Jem'Hadar hadn't found them yet. Kira realized she'd probably served as a distraction. They'd concentrated all their efforts on trying to find her.

After a brief reunion, Snoct hustled everyone into the storage bin and drove across the landing field. It was a tight fit, but nobody complained. Odo transformed himself into a cushion to take up less room. They all sat on him.

Kira weathered the bumpy ride in silence, as did the others. She didn't tell them how close she'd come to being captured, or that her personal cloaker had failed at a crucial moment, when it should have lasted another thirty seconds. She'd have something to say about *that* to Lieutenant Colfax when they got back to DS9.

Finally the ride ended. She felt the transport swing around, then back up. A second later the motor shut off.

Snoct opened the cargo bin. They'd pulled up by the hatch of the ship they'd taken to get here, Kira saw, exactly as he'd promised. She could have kissed him.

"It's ready to go!" Snoct said.

Odo and Worf hustled Orvor aboard.

"Thank you," Kira said. "I won't forget this, Snoct. If you ever make it to the Alpha Quadrant—"

"No, no!" he piped. "I will never leave Daborat V again!"

She laughed, then turned and dashed up the ramp. They'd spent too long here, she thought. She wanted to get home. Although the mission hadn't been a complete success, at least they'd rescued Orvor. That had to count for something. As they said during the Bajoran Resistance, any mission you came back from was a success.

She slid into the pilot's seat and powered up the engines. When Worf closed the hatch, she lifted off smoothly. The ship handled as well as ever, she found. They could be home in two days.

Suddenly the communicator gave a series of beeps. Ground control was hailing them.

"Odo!" she called.

"Right here," he said, appearing beside her. He activated the monitor.

"You are not cleared for takeoff," a Jem'Hadar warrior said.

"I'm leaving," Odo said. "Do nothing to stop me."

The Jem'Hadar opened his mouth, but nothing came out. He seemed to be struggling with an inner conflict. *Probably the orders another changeling gave him,* Kira realized with a grin. By the time he got it all sorted out, they'd be long gone.

She cleared the atmosphere and laid in a course for the wormhole. Forty-one hours, she thought, going to warp, and she'd be safe in her own bed.

She couldn't wait.

CHAPTER
28

As they emerged into the Alpha Quadrant through the wormhole, Major Kira saw that DS9 looked much the same as when she'd left. It hung before them, spinning slowly, its docking ring packed with ships. The *Excalibur* sat half a kilometer off from the station . . . probably waiting to take Orvor aboard, she thought. The Federation would doubtless be disappointed when they learned he hadn't managed to escape with the retrovirus, but she knew they'd get whatever he could remember from him. Perhaps it would provide a clue toward defeating the Jem'Hadar.

"Ten minutes," she called back.

Orvor grinned. "Thank you, Major."

In the two days since his rescue, he'd made an almost miraculous recovery, she thought. His burns had almost entirely healed, his yellow fur had taken on a rich luster, and his snout had turned a healthy pink. He didn't look like the same pathetic prisoner they'd rescued.

"DS9 to unidentified ship," Kira heard a familiar voice say over the subspace radio, "please identify yourself."

"This is Major Kira, Dax," she said. "We're coming home! Clear a berth for us."

"Docking Pylon three," Dax said. "Welcome home, Nerys!"

"Thanks," Kira said.

Sisko studied Kira and Worf, who both stood at attention before him.

All told, it had been quite a week, Sisko thought. An hour after Kira docked, Orvor had been bundled off aboard the *Excalibur* for a reunion with his mate. The *Excalibur* then put the captured Jem'Hadar ship in a tractor beam and towed it off for further study. Admiral Dulev would be a little disappointed about the retrovirus, but still, things could have gone much worse. The *Excalibur* had already taken the Valtusian ship aboard one of its docking bays. Although the changelings hadn't made many modifications to the ship beside adding tissue culture banks in which they had grown Valtusian skin—the same skin they'd used to fool Bashir's DNA scanner—Starfleet scientists would go over every inch of it. You never knew what might prove useful.

"Sir," Worf said, offering his report. Sisko accepted it, then took Kira's.

"I'll read them tomorrow," he promised. "Now, I think I'd like to buy you both drinks. From what I hear, you deserve them."

"If you don't mind my saying so," Kira said, "so do you. I hear you make quite an impressive Speaker, Captain."

"Well . . ." Sisko made a deprecating gesture. "One does what one must."

Grinning, he led the way out into Ops. Dax was just coming off her shift, he saw, so he invited her to join them, and she gladly accepted.

By the time they reached Quark's, their party had swelled to include Dr. Bashir, O'Brien, and Odo. Hopefully they'd find a table, Sisko thought, noting the time.

When he led the way inside, though, he found business decidedly slow. Half a dozen people sat at the Dabo tables, and only Morn sat at the bar nursing a drink. Other than that, the place was deserted.

Quark wandered over, looking a bit sour.

"What's wrong?" Sisko asked, looking around. "Where is everybody?"

"That's what I'd like to know," Quark grumbled. "You have one brawl, one terrorist attack, and one rumor of contaminated Bajoran spice ale—" Sisko noted the dark look Quark shot at Bashir, who shifted uneasily and didn't meet the Ferengi's gaze. There had to be a story there, Sisko thought. They'd worm it out of Bashir after he'd had a few drinks. "—and all of a sudden nobody wants to drink here anymore."

"They'll be back," Bashir said.

"They'd better," Quark said. "And don't think Vedek Werron isn't getting the bill for my lost business!"

"We need a table," Sisko said.

"Here," Quark said, leading them to a large one by the door. "Maybe people will notice you sitting here and come in."

Everyone began calling their orders. Quark hurried to fill them.

Yes, Sisko thought, it had been quite a week. A changeling plot had been foiled. An innocent Cardassian had been saved. And best of all, a Federation informant had been rescued, though Sisko had no idea if Orvor's information would prove useful. But best of all, his friends were alive and well and with him now.

"Drinks," he announced, "are on me."

He grinned. All in all, it had been a *very* good week, he thought.